ETERNAL SACRIFICE

A MORTAL ENCHANTMENT NOVEL

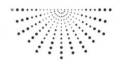

STACEY O'NEALE

I dedicate this book to my daughter, Madison O'Neale. You are the most beautiful part of my life.
I love you so much.

When sorrow comes, they come not single spies, but in battalions.

Hamlet Act IV, Scene V

PROLOGUE

PRISMA

18 years ago.

The pathway was about to implode.

Panic rippled through me in waves—no time to spare. My core fire kept the portal steady, but the attack slowly drained my energy. I had to run. It shouldn't be much farther. A series of screeching pops went off as cracks appeared on the interior of the tunnel. I had to go faster. Why was she doing this? For centuries, the water court had welcomed me. There was only one possible explanation: she knew I was coming and had foreseen the purpose of my visit. This attack only confirmed what I'd feared.

Britta chose a side.

His side.

Meeting the water queen in her territory was risky. Her power was strongest beneath the sea, surrounded by the magic of her element. As I fought my way through, my legs had begun to burn. I'd used too much of my power. That was likely her plan. She'd anticipated a confrontation and needed to make sure I wasn't at full strength. I'd hoped I could

1

reason with her. We were sisters. Queens of our courts. The best of friends.

And yet she'd conspired with my lover to end the life of our child.

A glowing light appeared. I'd reached the other side. Leaping toward the opening, I landed on my knees. I took a minute to catch my breath. When I stood, I studied my surroundings. It had been years since I'd been down here. I stared at the separate shimmering mist that kept the ocean water out. I imagined it was like living inside a sealed terrarium. Although this place resembled land, there were a few differences. It was always dark. Without the tiki torches lining the exterior, it would be pitch black. Air circulated freely, making it easy to breathe. Greenhouses filled with greenery and vegetation went on for miles.

Several water elementals passed through the mist. Each one transformed into a creature that looked similar to a mortal. They stood on two legs, but their skin remained scaled. The silence was deafening—no wind, rain, or storms. And all of the water elementals spoke using telepathy. In the distance, I spotted Britta's tower home. The creamy yellow bricks on the exterior of the castle looked like sand. Coral in a riot of colors served as decoration. A path made of crushed seashells led to the front gate.

As I approached, I'd expected guards to appear. I was sure Britta had attempted to close the pathway. She didn't want me here, yet no one came. My eyebrows furrowed as I made my way through the interior. I didn't see even a single elemental inside. It was unusual for the palace to be empty. Had she forced her kin into hiding when she realized I was coming? Was my friend so sure I'd attack? Or had she been persuaded?

I brushed it off for the moment.

There wasn't much furniture as I passed through hallways. The only decoration was the succession of beautiful paintings that lined my way. Each told the history of her court through the centuries, all the way back to the creation of the world.

Once I arrived at the end of the walkway, I headed up the stairwell. Britta's private quarters took up the entire uppermost floor of the tower. If she were still here, that was where she'd be. I reached the top and pushed two heavy wooden doors open.

Britta.

She stood on a stone balcony with her arms at her sides. Hanging tea lights illuminated the area, giving her ocean-blue, iridescent gown a sparkling hue. Flowing black hair poured down her back. The silvery tattoos on the sides of her face glowed as she gazed at the mist above our heads. I slowly moved closer, not forgetting that she had tried to prevent me from entering her realm. Her pupils were gone, eyes completely white. She was using her power to look into the future.

There was a buzzing in my head. Then I heard her voice. *"You should not have come, Prisma."*

I closed the distance between us. "You used your foresight without my permission."

"I did not seek him out. He brought him to me."

The Ring of Dispel, our sacred object, blocked my court from her visions. It wasn't a weakness she freely admitted, but I kept her secret. I wasn't fond of her premonitions. Some of her visions had caused more harm than good. "You had no right. He is my son."

Britta crossed her arms. *"Shielding this child will only lead to your demise."*

"I'm willing to die to protect any of my children."

Lowering her head, she replied, *"You will set events in motion that you cannot undo. This choice will be the end for us all."*

3

"Enough," I screamed. "I know why you tried to close the pathway. You've hidden what is mine somewhere within this castle."

"I will not allow you to stop him."

The sting of her betrayal pierced my heart. There was nothing left of our friendship. I was alone. "He stole our son." A fire ignited, burning in my core. "He's going to kill him."

"He will save us all by making the ultimate sacrifice." Her voice rose up an octave. It was a rare slip of emotion. *"Can you not see that?"*

"I *see* that my son is in danger," I sneered. "I *see* that you have betrayed me."

"You are in danger, sister. I sense darkness growing inside of you." She reached out to me like she was extending an olive branch. *"Let me help you."*

I pushed her hand away. She was correct. There was an anger building, but she was the cause. Britta had never gone against me. Not until now. "The only way you can help me is by returning my lover and my son to me."

Her eyes had become white once more. *"Evil remains hidden within your veil of protection. Lift the barrier. Together, we will identify the cause and rid the world of it."*

She made accusations against my son, turned my lover against me, and now she wanted more? "How could you think I'd even consider giving you entry into my court? Never."

"You have gone beyond reason."

Igniting a ball of fire in my hand, I ordered, "Bring them to me."

Her eyes flashed. *"You would use your power against me?"*

I watched as she called to the ocean. A stream of water shot out. I spun around, creating a swirling fire that wrapped around me. The burning heat turned her weapon into vapor.

As I extinguished the blaze, I glared at her. "There is nothing I wouldn't do to protect my child."

She blinked once, and her blue irises returned. *"Then, we are all lost."*

Why had it come to this? She was the one person I'd always counted on—my sister. Surely I could make her see my side. If there was even a shred of hope, I had to try. "It doesn't have to be this way."

Britta shook her head. *"I will play no further part in this."*

"You are the cause," I argued. "We're here right now because of your premonition. You have interfered where you shouldn't. Can you live with yourself if you're wrong?"

There was a long pause. *"If I had seen even one other possibility, I would not have shared my vision."*

Fire burst from my fingertips, encircling us into an inferno. The flames burned the stones we stood on. "I will kill the akasha myself if that's what it takes."

"That would be treason." Her voice remained calm.

"What about what you're doing?" I screamed. "You're trying to kill an innocent child."

Water rained over our heads, fighting the flames for control. *"One life in exchange for thousands is mercy."*

"I cannot let you do this," I replied. As I raised my hands, the circle of fire rose several feet.

"He is the destroyer." She took a step forward, trying to avoid the flames. Facing me, she blinked once. *"His whole life is in shadows. There is no other outcome for him."*

"You see possibilities. I know the future can change. You taught me that." I shook my head, sensing there was more to the vision than she was letting on. "I refuse to believe there is no hope for him."

"Every potential choice leads to devastation."

"I can stop this." All I had to do was alter what I'd planned. I swallowed the lump in my throat. Even if it broke my heart in the process, I'd do anything to prevent this. "I'll send him far away. Keep him out of my court. Out of Avalon, if necessary."

A tsunami appeared from the sea, creating waves as high as the castle. *"There is no way to prevent what will be."*

"He will not be harmed in any way. I won't allow it." With only one chance left, I tried to appeal to her heart. "You once loved a mortal as if he were your son. Thanks to me, you were able to raise him. You know what it feels like to be a mother. Can't you understand how I feel?"

The water calmed instantly, returning to its normal state.

Waving my hand, I extinguished my fire.

For the second time today, I saw a small bit of emotion on her face. Losing Lancelot had devastated her. It took centuries before she allowed anyone even to mention his name in her presence. *"I do understand your pain."*

"Then help me, sister." I gripped her shoulders, leveling our eyes. "We can save Rowan together."

CHAPTER ONE

ROWAN

K alin had to sacrifice herself?

Pain seared my chest, burning its way into my heart. I watched her mouth as she continued to speak. Words I didn't hear. The only sound in my ears was my heavy breath. I wasn't sure how long we sat motionlessly. Each one of us waited for the other to react. Frozen in a circle of marble chairs, we were seemingly unable to comprehend what Kalin had said. I met eyes with Britta, then Orion. I wanted desperately for one of them to say there was another solution. That this wasn't the only way, it couldn't be. Not after everything we'd been through together. Everything we'd lost.

I couldn't lose her too.

It had been eighteen months since I first saw her. Prisma sent me to kill her. She was supposed to be a danger to us all. Yet she seemed so fragile. More mortal than elemental. Untrained in her element and naive of the world that waited for her. There was no way I could end her life. I decided soon after that she needed to be protected. I'd keep her safe. If I were honest with myself, I'd admit my feelings for her started then. And now, I couldn't imagine my life without her. I loved her. How was I supposed to stand by and be okay with her decision?

I wouldn't. "You can't do this. I won't let you."

"It won't come to that, Rowan," Kalin replied. "I'm not going to wait for Valac to make a move. We'll strike first."

There was something different about her. Since she'd gained her akasha power, she spoke with a confidence I hadn't heard before. Her voice was stronger. Even her facial features had changed. Her cheekbones were more defined, while her lips were fuller. Even her eyes had changed. They were slightly larger, and the evergreen color was sharper. If I were seeing her for the first time, I would've never guessed she was half-mortal. It was as if her other half was gone. Perhaps it had something to do with her new power? Maybe it gave her an upgrade. Since I'd never met another akasha, there was no way to know for sure.

I smirked. "Sounds like you have a plan."

Orion cleared his throat, drawing everyone's attention to him. "I think we all need to step back and process this before we make a move against Valac."

I wasn't surprised by Orion's reluctance. He had joined with Jared and attacked the fire court, believing they had kidnapped King Taron. The desperation to save his best friend made him vulnerable. In addition to the loss of elemental lives, the four elements shifted out of balance. Natural disasters continued to wreak havoc all over the mortal world. We were spread too thin to keep them contained. Sadly, he could've avoided the devastation had he listened to reason. It was a decision he regretted more than any other.

"What are you suggesting?" I asked.

"We need to examine what we already know." He stood, pacing around us. "Valac has the Ring of Dispel and Excalibur. But Selene cannot be trusted. The fact that she came to us with this information makes me highly suspicious."

"What I told you was the truth," Selene argued, her face red with anger. "Valac wants to control all four courts. He will cut the mist if you don't surrender."

"Your word means nothing to me," Orion sneered.

Although Valac was the one that had kidnapped Taron, Selene supported him. Only minutes ago, Orion learned Sebastian killed Taron. The iron cuffs Valac used to imprison him had weakened his power. In his frail condition, he was only able to use his healing power to save Kalin's mother, Tricia. Judging by his clenched jaw and flared nostrils, Orion appeared as if he were moments away from attacking Selene.

I had to say something before this went any further. Selene was a lot of things and certainly deserved punishment, but she wasn't to blame for any of this. None of what had happened was her idea. She'd always been weak. "You could be right, Orion. I have more reasons to distrust her than any other. But I know Valac. He desires power more than anything else. That's why we need to focus on finding him."

He continued to glower at Selene. "And how are we going to do that, Rowan?"

"I can use my connection to the ring to sense its location." I approached Orion, putting my hand on his shoulder. "We can put an end to this if we get the sacred objects back. I agree with Kalin. We need to figure out his next move and attack first."

"You cannot defeat Valac," Britta announced, telepathically.

I turned around to face her. "Why not?"

Britta held up her palm, and a white light flashed in front of my eyes. When my vision returned, I stood on a flat field with miles of grass in every direction. I was no longer in the air court castle. At least, that was what I thought. It took me a couple of seconds to realize Britta had connected with my mind. She showed me a great battle. Hundreds of mortals fought all around, but no one noticed I was there. The men wore metal armor and rode horses. It looked like something out of a movie. My attention shifted to one knight emerging out of the crowd. He carried a large sword. One after another, he sliced into his opponents. The cuts he made didn't appear very deep, but each challenger instantly fell to the ground.

They were dead within seconds.

I heard Britta's voice in my head. *"As long as Valac wields Excalibur, he cannot be defeated. A small cut from its blade will kill you. Even the power of the akasha cannot save your life."*

There was another flash, and then I was back in the air court throne room. I glanced around, and everyone had their eyes on Britta. She must've shown each of us the vision. "Valac isn't much of a swordsman. He's much better at giving orders. I can take him."

Britta shook her head. *"Excalibur will increase his abilities. He will kill you, Rowan. No one will be a match for him."*

This situation had gone on long enough. My biggest regret was that I didn't let Taron put him to death when he had Prisma executed. At the time, I thought mercy was the best way to go. Give him a chance to redeem himself. But how many had lost their lives because of my sympathy? And now, it was Kalin's life in danger. It was time to end this. "He may have the sword, but I am the king of the fire court. The element is strongest in me. I will not lose."

"I have foreseen this exactly," Britta responded as she signaled something to the other water elementals. They nodded their heads and made their way toward the exit.

"What are you talking about?" I asked.

With her palm facing me, she replied, *"I will play no further part in this."*

She turned away and headed for the balcony.

"Where are you going?" I followed her.

"Back to my realm beneath the sea." She made her way toward the stone railing. The wind caught her hair, swaying her black waves like a flag. *"If this is to be our end, I will die defending my kin."*

As she leaped from the edge, her body liquefied into water. She landed on the ground with a splash. She headed right into a stream that ran down the side of the mountain. I no longer sensed her in my head.

Britta was gone.

I ran back into the room where everyone stood seemingly astounded by what they had witnessed. "Well, that was a dramatic exit."

"Has she abandoned the council?" Orion asked.

"There's nothing left of the high council," I shrugged. "I had hoped we'd reform it, but it looks like that's not going to happen."

Kalin came to stand in between Orion and me. "We'll find a way to bring her back, but for now, we need to focus on Valac."

The water queen's exit was a concern. What had she seen in her vision? She spoke as if she had to prepare her court for war. Questions swirled in my head, but I had to push them aside for now. Kalin was right. Finding Valac was the top priority.

"Rowan, can you sense the Ring of Dispel?" Orion asked, pulling me out of my thoughts.

Last time I tried, I needed Kalin and Britta's joined powers to find the ring. The three of us were successful, but it took a lot out of me. Without Britta, it would be even more difficult. My head still ached from the migraine. "It's not a constant connection," I said, massaging my temples. "I have to use my core energy to search for it."

"If you can tell us which territory he's in," Kalin added, "we should be able to anticipate his next move."

"I'll try." Closing my eyes, I focused on the image of the ring. Within my mind, a dark tunnel pulled me forward. Something slowly came into focus. It was greenery. I saw massive tree trunks, wild bushes, and a flat walkway like a path of some sort. I headed for the trail. Pain radiated from the back of my head, slowly spreading into my shoulders. My energy was fading. A hand slipped into mine, interlocking our fingers. It was Kalin. Within moments, our powers merged, and I felt an urgent jolt of incredible strength. Everything moved rapidly. It was as if someone had pressed the fast forward button in my head.

The location in the distance came into focus.

"He's at the edge of the woodland court," I shouted as I fell to my knees, exhausted from the power I'd used to find the ring. I locked eyes with Orion. "I'd guess he's heading for your castle."

"Valac sent you here to distract us." Orion went straight for Selene. "He knew about the summons."

"Marcus brought me against my will." Selene shrieked, trying to hide behind one of the hounds. "I had no control over that."

Marcus stood in front of Selene, blocking Orion. "Stay back," he ordered with a sharp tone in his voice. "This isn't the way to go."

"Marcus is right." I rushed in front of Orion before he could reach Marcus. His face was blood red. "You need to return to your court."

As my warning sunk in, terror flashed in Orion's eyes. "We have to stop him before he gets the Green Armor."

Britta's exit had sidetracked us. We should've anticipated he had spies everywhere. Someone had told him we were all here, leaving the woodland court open for the taking. I didn't want to leave Kalin. She was powerful, but she needed to learn to control it. Unfortunately, time was the one thing we never seemed to have. An ache settled in the pit of my stomach. As much as I hated it, I had no other choice. "I'm going with Orion. He will need all of the help we can give him."

"I'll prepare my guard," Orion announced.

"You're not going alone," Kalin said, signaling to one of her knights. "Go wake up your captain. I want no less than fifty knights to meet me at the woodland pathway in twenty minutes."

"Yes, my queen." The knight bowed and left.

"Thank you, Kalin," Orion said as he took Queen Marlena's hand and led her toward a side door.

"You're not going without me," Marcus added, shifting my attention to him.

I shook my head. "I need you to return home. You're the only one I trust to lead our court in my absence. The eternal flame must be protected."

Marcus sighed and then nodded. He didn't like my decision, but we both knew it was the right one. He tilted his head toward Selene. "What do you want me to do with her?"

"Take her with you." I leaned in, lowering my voice. "I get the feeling that she knows more than she's letting on. Maybe you can talk to her."

"You can't be serious," he snorted. "What makes you think Selene will talk to me?"

"You always managed to get through to me."

"She's not going to listen to me, Rowan." He glanced over at her. "You see the way she treats us. To her, we're nothing more than servants."

Marcus watched Selene fiddle with her skirts. She had a lot of nervous energy. Which only made me more suspicious. "All I'm asking you to do is try."

A low growl of frustration escaped his throat. "Don't do anything reckless."

"Me? Reckless?" I smirked. "Never."

He signaled to the other hounds. They grabbed Selene by the arms. She struggled as they exited out the same door as Orion. Once they were gone, I spun back around to face Kalin. We were alone once more. She stood with arms crossed, staring out into the distance. I'd seen that look before. She had a plan.

"I can't go with you," she said, with regret in her eyes. "If this is all a trick....If Valac comes here instead—"

"You have to protect your court." I ran my thumb over her cheek. She leaned into my touch. "I get it."

With determination in her tone, she said, "I want to make him suffer for what he's done."

I pulled her close, slipping my arms around her waist. "You're pretty hot when you get all riled up."

As she glanced up at me, I saw the worry in her eyes. She tried to hide it by looking away. I wasn't a fool. "Don't leave Orion's side," she said. "I can't lose anyone else."

I tucked a loose strand of hair behind her ear. "Are you all right?"

Lowering her head, she replied, "I'm not sure I'll ever be right again."

Kalin had been through so much over the past few months. She'd left her mother and the life she'd built in the mortal world only to discover her father was missing. She was thrust into power when he never fully recovered and then deceived by someone she trusted. She finally gained the power of the akasha but was too late to save Taron. Her pain and suffering were more than what most could bear. She was the strongest person I'd ever known. It was one of the many reasons I'd fallen in love with her.

"We're going to get through this." I cupped her face in my hands. "Together."

"I know." A cool breeze flowed through the room, rustling the ends of her red hair. She faked a smile. "We'd better get going. Orion has to prepare his court."

I took her hand in mine and led her outside. The sun was at its highest. For most, the day had just begun. The morning dew had settled on each blade of grass like tiny emeralds. Only a few of the air court elementals roamed the courtyard. At this elevation, the mountain air was crisp and cool. The clouds floated all around us. Under normal circumstances, it would've been a beautiful day to fly.

But things were about as far from normal as they could get.

When we arrived at the pathway, Orion and Marlena were deep in discussion. Air court knights were everywhere. Kalin left to find their captain. When Orion noticed me, he nodded. I watched as he signaled to one of his knights. With their swords drawn, the royal guard encircled the king and queen. They formed a barrier around them. Once they were inside the pathway, clusters of air court knights followed.

After the last of them were gone, Kalin stood alone by the swirling entryway. "Promise you'll come back to me. I need to hear the words."

"I promise," I said, wrapping my arms around her. I lowered my mouth, and our lips brushed together. It started soft, but it quickly escalated—all the worry over losing her morphed into uncontrollable need. I pulled her closer, curling my fingers around the belt loops of her jeans. For a minute, I lost myself in the kiss.

I loved her. More than anything. More than myself. If we didn't succeed, I'd lose her. As the only akasha in over a hundred years, she was the one elemental who had the power to stop Valac once the mist was punctured. Her blood sealed the hole. All of her blood. Her life. The ultimate sacrifice. No, I wouldn't let that happen. I abruptly released her from my embrace, and she gasped in surprise.

Putting space between us, I unsheathed my sword. "This ends today."

CHAPTER TWO

KALIN

The akasha was absolute.

Both loved and feared—the strongest of all of the elementals with control over the four elements. I possessed immeasurable power and knowledge that had been passed down through the centuries. I was the beginning and end to it all. And I'd been given one central purpose: protect the mortals by keeping the elements in balance. But why me? I wasn't even a full elemental. The only halfling akasha in our history. Why was I chosen?

I'd spent most of my life preparing for my duties. I left the only life I'd known in the mortal world, at sixteen years old, to ascend to the throne and become the queen of the air court. Avalon was supposed to be the picturesque realm my father had described. The peaceful place was full of magical creatures that controlled the elements of nature.

Promises made never came to be.

Instead, I found myself thrust into a world in turmoil, on the brink of war. My father was missing, and I was forced to navigate my new home without him. I was untrained in my air element and naïve to all the politics that went along with being a member of the royal family. Had it not been for Rowan and Ariel, I would've never survived. Mistakes happened along the way, and we didn't succeed in preventing the war. Many lives were lost.

My father was one of them.

Not long after his death, the full power of the akasha surged through me. I killed the elemental that had betrayed us and claimed the throne. I wish I could say that was the end of it all, but the worst was yet to come. Thanks to his twin sister Selene, we now know Valac's plan. He wanted to use the stolen artifacts to claim control over all four territories. If we did not relinquish our courts to him, he threatened to cut the mist that protected Avalon—a move that would kill thousands within days.

Only the blood of the akasha could seal the hole.

I refused to believe that was my only purpose. I was more than a sacrifice. After what I had survived, I wouldn't let this be the end. I was going to figure out why I had this power bestowed on me. When I first became the akasha, thousands of pages of information rushed into my mind. It seemed nearly impossible to sort through it all. I needed to read through the akasha journals one by one. There had to be another way to stop Valac. Something we could use to vanquish the power of these sacred objects.

And I was going to discover it.

Staring at the pathway, I feared for Rowan. In only eighteen years, he had been through enough anguish to last a lifetime. He carried a weight he doesn't deserve. Somehow, he held himself responsible for all that happened with Valac. As many times as I tried to convince him otherwise, he believed it was his duty to end his madness. My stomach twisted in knots as I worried that the burden he put on himself would make him careless. Valac was much stronger now that he had Excalibur. I prayed Rowan could push aside the obligations he felt, and make smart choices. I didn't want to imagine living in this world without him.

Every day we were together, I'd fallen more in love with him.

I shuffled my way back into the castle. I assumed my mother was still asleep. At least, I hoped she was. She'd been inconsolable since my father's death. He'd sacrificed his own life to save hers. It must've been agony for her, watching him die. Tears lined my eyelids. I brushed them away with the back of my hand. Since she wasn't at the meeting, she had no idea what had happened. I asked one of my guards to bring her to me along with any of my father's ashes that remained.

Although elementals didn't perform funerals—there was nothing left to bury—I had to do something to honor him. He hadn't been honest with me for most of my life, but he truly thought he was protecting me. And I loved him with all of my heart. Very little time had passed, yet I already felt his absence. Losing him had broken me. Time supposedly healed the wound, but I wasn't sure. Sebastian murdered him, ripping him away from Mom and me. Essentially robbing us of the family we had waited so long to reunite. How would I ever come to terms with that?

A question I imagined I'd contemplate for the rest of my life.

"Kalin, what's going on?"

I turned around. Mom stood in the courtyard with her arms wrapped around her waist. Her red hair was disheveled, and her eyes swollen from many hours' worth of tears. My chest tightened. It was painful to see her like this. Had I been stronger, I could've protected my father and saved her from the pain of his loss. But I was the one who was deceived by Sebastian. I believed he was my friend, and that he had the best interests of our court in mind. It was foolish. A mistake I'd never be able to take back.

I held out my hand. "Come join me out here."

"One of your guards said to give this to you." She placed a gold thimble in my palm. The contents of the tiny container were all I had left of him. "What is it?"

"Dad's ashes." I waited until her evergreen eyes met mine. "I thought maybe we could have a private ceremony to say goodbye. If it's too much, we can wait."

"No, I think it's perfect," she replied sniffling. "We both need to do this."

We headed to the highest stone balcony in the castle. From here, we could see the clouds beneath us. The sun warmed our faces. It was perfect weather. If Dad were here, he'd be outside enjoying the day with members of our court. They loved him so much. Since the news of his death, each smiled and tried to carry on as he would've wanted. But the pain of his loss and the fear of the unknown was felt by all of us. He'd been their leader since the beginning. I was sure they all had their concerns.

"Let's do this together," I said.

With our hands joined, I held the thimble above our heads. A sizzle of power ran up my arm and into my fingertips. Air thrust the ashes out of the container, casting them into the wind. We watched the remains as they joined the skies. Seconds later, they were gone. I imagined part of my father would float around Avalon forever. I glanced over at Mom. Streams of tears ran down both her cheeks. "What should we say?"

"Whatever's in your heart," she replied.

I paused for a moment. "I wish we'd had more time, Dad. But I'm grateful for the weeks we spent together. I promise I will take care of our court." My throat tightened, and I swallowed hard. "I won't let you down."

Mom pulled me into a hug. We embraced for a long while, crying on each other's shoulders. After a few minutes, she released me. "Goodbye, my love," Mom said into the wind. "I know we will be reunited someday. I love you with all of my heart."

I put my arm around her, and she tilted her head onto my shoulder. She'd always been the strongest person. To see her truly fall apart was agony. She tightened her grip on my waist, leaning her weight into me. For the first time in my entire life, I was the one holding her together.

"I SHOULD GO," ARIEL SAID, EYES NERVOUSLY ROAMING THE room.

The highest-ranking elementals attended the council meetings in our court. This group made all the decisions about daily life. Some members had been on the council for centuries. Others had replaced older relatives who no longer wished to participate. It was considered the greatest honor to be part of such a regal group. Ariel had previously never been invited to attend, so I understood why she felt uncomfortable. "No," I replied, the corners of my lips turned up. "I need you to be here."

I'd asked the staff to put something casual together in the throne room. With everything going on, I wanted to keep things simple. I should've known that wasn't possible for elementals, even in the air court. When I first entered the room, I saw that a mahogany wood rectangular table had been set up, with matching chairs. An exotic fruit and cheese centerpiece took up most of the table, along with long-stemmed crystal glasses filled with red wine. Small ceramic plates, napkins, and utensils took up the remaining space. I sat down at the head of the table and motioned for Ariel to sit next to me.

The council members arrived soon after. They wore their

yellow ceremonial robes. It was no wonder why I stood out among them. I was the only one without wheat-blond hair and pale blue eyes. One by one, they glanced at Ariel with perplexed brows. Not a single one questioned why she was here. Since my akasha power ignited, their attitude toward me had changed substantially. They were courteous and polite. None of them had challenged me in any way. I'd finally received the respect from them that I should've had from the beginning.

It was a long time coming.

I wasted no time with pleasantries. As soon as they all were seated, I made them aware of Valac's plan, the attack we anticipated on the woodland court, and our need to mobilize our knights. The emotions were mixed. We were all still mourning my father's death. Many on the council had been close friends.

One of the older female council members stood. "What happens if Valac succeeds? Are we prepared for that?"

"If Valac cuts the mist, my blood will seal the incision." Many of them relaxed after hearing my words. "But it will mean that I have to sacrifice myself. Which is why I've called this meeting."

"What do you mean?" she asked, sitting back in her seat.

I stood. "If I die, I want to appoint Ariel as my successor."

Several of them gasped. Whispers broke out among the group. None objected. I glanced over at Ariel. Her eyes were wide and focused on me. The complete and utter shock spread across her face told me everything I needed to know. Because her mouth was open, I waited for her to say something. A minute went by, and no words came out.

"I guess I should've asked you first." I tugged at her arm until she stood. With my hands clasped around her biceps, I asked, "Do you accept?"

Shaking her head, she replied, "I don't even want to think about you dying."

"Trust me." It wasn't something I wanted to think about either. "I'm going to do everything I can think of to avoid it. But in case I have to sacrifice myself, I need to know our court moves forward with the right elemental."

She met eyes with each of the council members. I noticed a few jealous scowls as well as a few frightened faces. "I don't know."

"Ariel, you can do this." She stared back at me like a deer caught in headlights. "You're the only person I trust to do this. You're one of the strongest people I've ever met, and I know you'll be a great queen."

"This is a formality, right?" She swallowed hard. "I mean, you don't think Valac will succeed?"

"Yes, we'll find a way to stop him," I answered firmly. I wasn't as sure as I sounded, but I believed it was possible. I had to exude confidence in front of my court. In times of war, they needed a strong leader they could follow. It was the only way we were all going to get through this.

Ariel let out a sigh of relief. "Okay then, I accept the position."

A few unenthusiastic claps broke out. I ignored them. Now that I'd made my formal announcement, there was nothing they could do to stop it. Beaming, I pulled Ariel into a hug. "Thank you."

As I was about to sit back down, she grabbed my arm. "Do me a favor."

I raised an eyebrow. "What?"

She squeezed my hand. "Don't die."

CHAPTER THREE

ROWAN

My muscles burned in anticipation of the battle.

The portal opened about a mile away from the woodland caves. If the attack had already begun, we didn't want them to see us coming. The faeries were likely fighting them around the exterior of the caves. It would've been better for us to come in from behind so that two forces were hitting them from different directions. With that strategy, we had a chance to surround them. That would've prevented any planned retreat, and we'd eliminate them once and for all.

But first, we had to get there.

I gripped my sword tightly as I scanned our surroundings. I wasn't going to take the chance that we might be surprised. The vision I saw was clear. Valac stood on the edge of the woodland territory with an army of his own. We already knew he was coming for the Green Armor. According to legend, no one could defeat the person who wore the enchanted metal. An entire army could attack all at once, and it wouldn't matter. The armor would still protect the wearer.

Orion and Marlena remained at the front of our group, surrounded by their guard. The air court knights made up the cluster in the middle. I remained in the back, giving me the best view. Twigs broke beneath our feet as we marched through the thick brush. Lush greenery surrounded us in every direction. The forest was eerily silent. That meant either nothing was happening or something had already happened, and everyone had fled. But it wasn't like the woodland faeries to run away.

They were much too plucky for that.

Branches in the trees above our heads rustled as a strong wind current blew through. I kept my eyes on the tall, twisted tree trunks as we passed by. Valac could've had soldiers hidden nearby. Many elementals could fly, making an air assault a possibility. I wouldn't put anything past him at this point. The rumor going around was that he had supporters from each of the courts. The more power he gained, the more elementals questioned the supremacy of the royal families. Fearful of the future, some had joined his side.

The unbalanced elements had wreaked havoc in the mortal world. Natural disasters at peak levels ravaged every corner of the Earth. Earthquakes in Asia. Hurricanes in the Caribbean islands. Sandstorms in the Middle East. Tornadoes in the center of North America. No place was safe. Elementals from every court continued to fight them back, but we're spread thin. The only way to save our planet from extinction was to realign the four primary elements.

The group came to an abrupt stop, and I nearly knocked over the knight in front of me.

Above the treetops, dark, billowy clouds of smoke filled the skies. I wasn't able to see where they were coming from, but I had an idea. A jolt of power surged through my arms, racing down into the tips of my fingers. I'd run to the top of the hill looking for Orion. He had his arm around Marlena as they watched something in the valley below. I settled next to him. To my horror, it was as I had feared.

The massive flesh-colored caves were on fire. Smoke barreled out of the cut-out doors and windows. The scent of ash burned my nostrils. Knights fought on the ground and spread into the caves. Iron weapons clashed together. The ground shook as the faeries used their magic to defend themselves. Flying fire elementals flew over top the battle, burning the small pixies as they attempted to extinguish the flames. Their bellowing screams could be heard even from this far away. Blood and corpses lay everywhere. The woodland fae certainly didn't go down without a fight.

My first instinct was to run right through the warfare, killing every fire elemental who crossed my path. My core fire burned beneath my skin, begging to be released. But I wasn't the king of this territory. Orion had to be the one to signal the assault. "What is your command?" I asked.

Rage had made his face blood-red. "Ready your weapons," he ordered.

"My pleasure," I replied, igniting a ball of fire in my palm. The knights formed two lines behind us with an iron sword in one hand and a shield in the other. They awaited his cue.

Orion's expression hardened as he raised his hands in the air. The dirt beneath our feet rose from the ground, forming large cones that twisted in the air like tornadoes. I had to use my arm to shield my eyes. There had to be two or three dozen of them, each the size of a small car. Growling, he thrust his hands forward. One by one, the large gravel funnels knocked the fire elementals out of the sky.

"Attack," he screamed as he rushed toward the caves.

As we raced down, we caught the attention of several fire elementals. They headed toward us. I ran in front of our group with my sword above my head. One elemental broke out in front of the pack, rushing straight at me. He'd made a grave mistake. Our swords made a loud screeching sound as they scraped together. I threw a fireball into his face. A fire wouldn't kill a member of my court, but it would distract him. As he attempted to brush the flames away, I spun around and sliced right through his middle. His blood dripped down my blade.

Air court knights used their wind magic to clear a walkway to the caves' entrance. As we fought our way through the battle, I tried to stay as close as I could to Orion. I had no idea where he kept the Green Armor. He had hundreds of rooms to choose from within these caverns. If I had any hope of getting to Valac, I had to stay with him. But Valac's rogue elementals never let up. The rumors were true. He had members of every court fighting on his side. I couldn't even imagine what he'd promised them.

Staying close to Orion, I lined up with a few of his guards that he'd brought with him. Most had remained with Marlena at the top of the mountain. Rather than worry about her safety, he chose to keep her away from the battle. We moved toward the main entrance of the caves. I created a circle of fire around us. The blaze kept most of the elementals away. However, members of my court sauntered right through the flames. Each time one of them stepped out of the inferno, I'd slit his throat. It reminded me of the whack-a-mole game I liked to play at the mortal arcade. After more than twenty minutes of fighting, I'd lost count of how many rogues had made friends with the sharp end of my blade.

Smears of blood covered most of my clothes by the time we reached the heavy wooden door. Orion waved his hand over the golden knob, and it slowly creaked open. We entered the main foyer with his guard. The air knights had been ordered to remain outside to prevent anyone from following us. We stepped over bodies in various stages of decomposition. My heart ached for my friend. Seeing so many of his faeries lying dead at his feet must've been torturous. Had I not been betrayed by the rogue fire elementals, I imagined I'd feel the same way.

Orion remained silent as we hurried through several winding hallways, and then multiple sets of stairs. Our shoes thumped against the gold marble flooring. Gold wallpaper covered every walkway we passed. Golden sconces bejeweled with multi-colored stones illuminated our way. Even the candles were gold. But nothing surprised me. I'd always known that the woodland court was the most lavish of the four. It seemed that they reveled in the extravagant.

By the time we stopped, I had guessed we were about a quarter-mile beneath the surface. Orion placed his hand on a wall. He moved his palm as if he were drawing a symbol. When he stepped back, a shimmering golden door appeared. One of his guards reached for the knob and held the door open. Several of his knights entered, making sure it was safe for him. When they nodded, we made our way inside.

We stood inside another massive, oval-shaped cave. Golden chandeliers hung from the high ceiling. Each one held large, rectangular candles that lit the entire room. The interior matched the flesh-colored exterior of the caves. Walls lined with bookcases packed to the brim with books. There had to be thousands of them. Other areas had iron weapons displayed. Some had to be hundreds of years old. On the furthest wall, a single chair sat in the corner with a woven blanket slung over the top. Right above, hung a painted portrait of the king and queen.

Orion made his way over to a wall with gold metallic inlay. The thick metal was shaped into a huge door but didn't appear to have any way to open it. My eyebrows snapped together as he pulled a small blade out of his side pocket and made a tiny incision on the pad of his index finger. A thin line of blood dripped into his palm. He pressed his hand into the wall. The area around the trimming cracked, and a cloud of dust cloaked the area. Fragments of the wall crumbled to the ground in large pieces. He stepped over the chunks of rubble, entering the hole he'd made.

Gasps filled the cave as Orion returned, holding a flat metal board. Resting on top were several pieces of forest green armor. As I got closer, I noticed the metal had etchings all over the exterior. Some of the markings were Celtic, while others appeared to be words from a language I didn't recognize: something ancient, no doubt. Every elemental in the room swarmed around Orion, each eager to see what most had thought was nothing more than a legend. Only the members of the royal families knew about the sacred objects and their power. Considering what he had gone through to get the armor, I'd bet he had it in here for centuries.

"Thank you, Orion."

I whirled around. Valac held Excalibur in his hand. Blood dripped down the blade. Four of the woodland personal guards were dead beneath his feet. Each had been sliced open at the neck. They had already begun to decompose. Heat surged through my body as I released my sword from its sheath. "I've been looking for you."

"Sorry, I'm late. I wasn't exactly sure where Orion had hidden the armor." Valac chuckled. "It was so nice of you to lead the way."

"Valac, you can't do this," Orion said, positioning himself in front of me. "Cutting the mist will kill thousands, including you. You have to stop this ridiculous quest."

"Pledge your allegiance, Orion," Valac replied. "Turn over your court to me, and I'll end this right now."

"This is about control of the woodland court?" Orion asked as a line etched between his eyebrows.

"Yes," he replied. "The woodland court … along with all of the other courts."

"Haven't you seen what the unbalanced elements have done to the mortal world?" Orion screamed, causing the metal armor in his arms to clink together. "The planet is being destroyed by this war. One elemental cannot rule over all four courts. There has to be an equal balance."

"You're an old fool, Orion." Valac shook his head. "The courts *can* be balanced under one ruler. That's the only way to be sure the balance remains."

Valac's rogue elementals entered the room one by one until they lined the walls. Most of them were fire court, but there were plenty from the other courts. The color had drained from Orion's face as he recognized the members of his court that had betrayed him. We were outnumbered five to one. Anger churned in my stomach. I snarled at Valac. "Why don't you fight me for the armor?" I said, pointing the tip of my sword at him. "Show your followers what kind of a leader you truly are."

"Gladly," he replied, sneering at me. "I've waited a long time for this."

I waved him over. "Take your shot."

The crowd of rogues cheered as we circled each other like two lions fighting over control of their pride. I had to fight the urge to charge him. Excalibur made him much too dangerous for that. No, I had to take him down with my sword. Valac and I had sparred when I was a child. Even then, he wasn't much of a challenge. I flexed my shoulders as if I were about to lunge. He jolted in response. He might've had a powerful weapon, but he still feared me.

"No," Orion interrupted, turning both our heads to his direction.

"What are you doing?" I barked, heading toward him.

"You can take it, Valac." Orion handed the armor to one of the rogue elementals. He ran it over to Valac, who seemed stunned by his surrender. "Please, leave."

"You surprise me, Orion," Valac said, examining each piece of the armor. When he was satisfied, he signaled to his followers. They headed out the door behind him. A smile danced on his lips. "See you around."

I stood still, dumbfounded. What happened? Had Orion declared defeat? Did he think he was saving the remaining members of his court? When I attempted to chase after Valac, a muscular arm pulled me back. It was Orion. "What are you doing?" I asked, attempting to release my arm from his grip. "I'm not going to let him have it. You know what this means."

"I had to let him go, Rowan." He put his hand on my shoulder and squeezed. "All he needed to do was cut you with Excalibur, and you're dead. I wasn't going to stand here and watch that happen."

I crossed my arms. "Valac would be dead before he got the chance."

Shaking his head, he replied, "I wasn't willing to risk your life."

"I had a plan," I argued.

He raised an eyebrow. "Really? What was your plan?"

I opened my mouth, then closed it. Was he right? I paused. My entire focus had been on killing Valac. But I was in such a rush to get over here I'd never actually planned anything out. Orion was right. Had he not stopped me, I'd likely be dead. "What are we going to do now?"

"The armor was our only hope." He strode over to the chair and sat down. His elbows were balanced on his knees while his head rested in his hands. "The armor was strong enough to withstand a blow from Excalibur, giving us a chance to get the sword away from him. Now, I'm not sure what we can do."

A vision of Kalin floated into my head along with an idea. "What about the shield?"

He glanced up at me. "The shield is protected by strong

magic. It has enough power to equal Excalibur. But the armor protects the entire body. Only the most skilled warrior could use that shield against the sword."

"I'll carry the shield." It made perfect sense. I finally had a way to keep Kalin safe. If I had the shield, he'd have no reason to attack the air court. My belly filled with anticipation. I clenched my fists at my sides. "Let him come for me."

Orion paused for several moments. "Are you sure that's what you want to do?"

Until we found a way to stop Valac, I had no other choice. "It's our best option."

"If this is your plan, the woodland court is with you." He stood firm. "What do you need from me?"

"I must return to the air court. Kalin needs an update." I wasn't sure if she'd go along with my plan, but I had to make her see this was the best way. I refused to sit around, waiting for another attack. We had to make a stand. "In the meantime, we're going to need iron weapons and as many knights as you can spare."

"Give me two days." He nodded and held his arm out. We shook hands. "You'll have everything you need."

CHAPTER FOUR

KALIN

Several hours had passed since Rowan left.

After the funeral for Dad, and the meeting with the council, I needed a little time by myself. Too much had happened, and I still didn't feel like I'd wrapped my head around it all. I wanted to go somewhere quiet. Somewhere outside of the castle. I headed down to the spot where the woodland portal had opened. It stood on a flat surface on the side of the mountain. I sat down and ran my hand across the moss green silky strands. Grass on Avalon was so soft it almost felt fake.

A sound like thunder jolted me to my feet. Winds collected, swirling together like a tornado. I stepped backward. Someone was about to come through the pathway. A bunch of leaves and branches blew out of the portal. Then Rowan burst out. A moment of relief quickly dissipated once I got a good look at him. His shirt was torn in several spots and scorched with burn marks. A spray of dried blood covered most of his cheek and the hair above his ear. I ran to him and locked my arms around his neck. All I could smell was the scent of charred ash. "I was so worried. Are you all right?"

He wrapped his arms tightly around my waist, burying his face in the crook of my neck. "I'm okay. I swear."

"I'm having a hard time believing you." I released him from my embrace, needing to examine him further. He looked like he stepped out of the final scene in a horror movie. "Were you able to stop Valac?"

"How did you know I'd be here?" he asked, ignoring my question.

"I didn't." Scanning his body, I searched for injuries. "What happened to you?"

"Valac has the armor." He ran his fingers through his tousled hair. "But we have a plan. I need you to take me to the shield."

"What? Why?" As he strode toward the castle, I shook my head. What happened? I got that this was an emergency, but he was gone all day. Now he was here with no real explanation, drenched in blood. Was it his, or had he done this to someone else? Had there been a battle? Were many elementals killed? He offered no details except that he wanted the shield. Needing to know more, I caught up to him and grabbed his arm. "Slow down and tell me everything that happened."

He let out an exaggerated breath. "We don't have enough time. Valac could already be on his way. I need to get the shield out of here. Away from you."

Had he decided that I couldn't protect the shield? Maybe that was true when I first arrived in Avalon, but now I was different. The strongest elemental. "I'm the akasha," I reminded him. "I can handle myself."

"I know how powerful you are," he smirked. "I also know that Valac can kill you with a paper cut from that sword. I won't take a chance like that. Not with you."

His protective words were a sweet gesture, but nothing was going to sway me. I still had unanswered questions. "What are you planning to do with the shield?"

He grimaced.

I crossed my arms and raised an eyebrow.

When he figured out I wasn't going anywhere until he filled in the blanks, he replied, "I'm taking the shield to my court." I still didn't move. A muscle in his jaw twitched. "The shield is one of the few pieces of armor that can withstand a blow from Excalibur. He'll come for it."

He wanted to take the shield to the fire court so Valac would follow him. What was the advantage of that? Valac knew his court as well as Rowan. Maybe better. "And when he does?"

"I'll challenge him," he replied sternly. "If I'm quick enough, I'll be able to get the sword away from him. The hounds will be there to finish him off."

What if he couldn't get the sword away from Valac? He would die. My chest tightened at the thought. "No, Rowan. I can't let you do that. I'm not going to risk your life."

His expression hardened. "But it's okay for you?"

Yes, it was. I might not have fully understood all of my powers, but I knew my core purpose. My duty was to balance the elements. I had to keep the mortal world safe. "I'm the akasha. It's what I was meant to do."

"No, it's not." The corners of his mouth turned up as he cupped my face. "You're *meant* to rule the air court. You're *meant* to live a long and happy life. But since you've been here, you've had pieces of that life chipped away bit by bit. And after everything you've been through, I refuse to stand back and allow you to sacrifice your life too."

"I'm not giving up." I put my hands over the top of his, slowly lowering them. "But if we can't stop him. If there's no other way—"

"There has to be." He rubbed the back of his neck. "Maybe we're missing something. In the akasha journals, did they mention anything about the creation of the mist?"

All of the information from the journals imported into my mind moments after I received my akasha powers. Thousands of pages of information all at once. It was impossible to remember every last detail. But maybe if I focused on the creator of the mist. Maybe I could pull it up like a file on a computer. I closed my eyes, concentrating on the mist. In my vision, the mist shimmered with a riot of colors. For a moment, its immense power flowed through me. My skin hummed. As the mental pages flipped, I tried to center all my energy on the creator. Every second I held on drained me. Trying to search my mind used up a lot of my strength. My knees wobbled, and I was about to collapse when muscular arms wrapped around me. As I lowered to the ground into a sitting position, I opened my eyes. Rowan was bent down in front of me.

"What's wrong?" he asked, as his expression softened.

This method wasn't going anywhere. I couldn't access the information without exhausting myself. With Valac gaining momentum, I had to conserve my strength. "I think it would be better if I searched through the actual journals. Using my power like this weakens me."

"Where are the journals?"

I'd kept them in my room for weeks while I was trying to read them. But once I gained my powers, I decided it was best to store them with the rest of the sacred texts and artifacts. It seemed like the safest place. Very few were aware they existed. Only the kings and queens of the courts knew where they were and how to get there. "In the caverns below the castle."

He smiled. "Lead the way, Jelly Bean."

I shook my head. "Are you ever going to stop calling me that?"

"Nope."

The vaults could only be accessed using a portal. Each court had its own. The fire court entrance was somewhere in the castle. I doubted Rowan knew where it was. Dad told me no one outside of the air court could use our portal. I had one other option. The journals said akasha could create portals. Once inside the pathway, I could control where I wanted to go. It wasn't something I'd ever tried before. Now seemed like a good time to give it a go. I closed my eyes. With my palms out, I motioned my hands around in a circle.

"What are you doing?" Rowan asked, cautiously.

"You'll see." Slowly, I increased the size of the circle until it was large enough for us to walk through. When I opened my eyes, a shimmering golden tunnel swirled a few feet in front of us.

"Holy shit," he said, staring at my creation with wide eyes. "Did you create a portal?"

"An akasha portal." I corrected, feeling pretty impressed with myself.

He approached the pathway, touching the rim with the tips of his fingers. "My girlfriend is a total badass."

"Come on." I laughed as I grabbed his hand and tugged him inside.

When we reached the end of the tunnel, we stood in total darkness. Before I could say anything, Rowan snapped his fingers. A baseball-sized orb of blue fire swirled inches above his open palm. He smirked. No matter what happened, he never seemed to lose his sense of humor. Or his cockiness. I reached for a torch I saw on the ground, and he lit it. The area around us illuminated enough to see that the limestone caverns were miles wide. Stalactites hung down like icicles, while thick columns supported the vast ceilings.

"This place is incredible," Rowan said, taking in the scenery.

It was obvious by his reaction that he'd never been here. I wasn't surprised. His mother shared very little with him. Pain and torture had been her only gifts. As we walked through the arena-sized caverns, the wind stirred all around us. It was the first wind—the remains of all of the air elementals who eventually found their way down here. Their presence gave me a surge of power. The last time I was here, I remembered it felt chilly. Now it was warm and seemed to wrap around me like an embrace. For a second, I held on and imagined it was my father. I sensed he was with me.

After a few minutes of walking, we reached the silver vault-like door with the air court symbol embedded into it. I ran my hand over the seal. A rumbling filled the silence, and then the door slowly creaked open. Rowan motioned his hand for me to lead the way. I watched him as he took in the rows of dark wood shelves that lined the walls with hundreds of leather-bound books.

"What is this place?" he asked as he studied the space.

"It's where all the sacred texts are stored. The complete history of the elementals is down here. Anything and everything you've ever wanted to know." I waved my hand. "All in one secret place."

He stared at one of the bookshelves that had the fire court symbol embedded into the top. "Who knows about this place?"

Dad said only the kings and queens knew, and they couldn't share the information until they passed on the throne to the next ruler. "Dad, Orion, Marlena, Britta, and probably your mom and aunt."

The stacked akasha journals were on the small marble table in the middle of the massive room. I sat down in one of the four chairs while Rowan continued to tour the rest of the library. Once he reached the far end, he stopped at the glass octagon-shaped display that housed the Shield of Lancelot. He opened the encasement. When he held it, the shield flashed a bright white light.

"I can feel its power," he said, rubbing his hand over the smooth surface. He traced his finger over the three diagonal red bands. "It's radiating into me, making me stronger."

As fierce as he already was, the weapon made Rowan lethal. "Dad told me it will increase your strength three times more than you are right now."

"Incredible."

While Rowan focused on the shield, I skimmed through the journals. When I first tried to read them, they were in a language Dad didn't recognize. Since I gained my power, I understood every word. I sat for hours reading page after page. Their journals weren't in chronological order. Each akasha wrote about their own experiences. Some detailed the history of the elementals, but most were concerning the everyday tales of the ones that came before me.

I learned that I could drain an elemental of their power. It could be used to weaken an elemental or remove it permanently. Fourteenth-Century akasha wrote about a few water elementals that had misused their powers. The sirens sang to lure mortal men into the water, and then they drowned them for their amusement. This particular akasha removed their powers and banished them from Avalon. They were unable to transform out of their fish form and lived a short lifespan.

I discovered a passage referencing the creation of the mist —a short paragraph. Anticipation rippled through me as I read. I couldn't help smiling when I saw the name. A name I recognized from my mortal mythology books. I was surprised I'd never guessed. "Merlin is the creator," I announced with excitement.

He sprung to his feet. "Where can we find him?"

"I don't know. The journals are incomplete."

Rowan stared out into the distance, rubbing his hand over his knuckles. "I might know another way."

My eyebrows furrowed.

"When I went to the eternal flame, I spoke to the original elders of my court." He held out his hand, helping me to my feet. "They might be able to tell me where I can find Merlin."

The elders had given Rowan back his wings. Based on what he'd told me, they seemed to be aware of everything that had happened in Avalon over the centuries. I sensed they would know about the power of the mist and its creator. "Is it dangerous?"

He shrugged. "No, I don't think so."

"If you think they'll help, you should go." I wished I could've gone with him. But I couldn't leave my court. "I'll stay here and continue to search through the journals."

He pulled me against his chest. "I don't want to leave you again."

"I don't want you to leave either." My heart ached. After everything, leaving him again was the last thing I wanted to do. "But it doesn't seem like we have much choice." As he tilted my chin upward, our eyes met. He pressed his lips gently against mine. It was odd at first. Rowan was so intense I almost expected a rough kiss. But this was sweet and full of emotion. The kind of kiss that made toes curl and butterflies dance all over your skin. I opened my mouth, and his tongue slipped inside. He tasted like cinnamon. His arms tightened around my waist, removing any space left between us. The world around us faded away, and all I could feel was him. I prayed the moment would never end.

A whimper escaped my throat as he pulled away.

He smirked. "I have to stop, or I'll never leave."

"I know." My cheeks warmed. "I feel the same way."

We both knew what was at stake. But, selfishly, I wanted

to keep Rowan with me. We'd spent so much time apart. Any time we managed to get together, something always separated us. I longed for those days we spent at the beach when we first met. All those hours we'd trained and talked. Well, I'd mostly asked questions he hadn't answered. The corners of my mouth curved into a smile. I'd fallen in love with him during that time. He'd saved my life more than once. It seemed like he was by my side with every step I'd made. I owed him my life several times over.

I made my way over to the shield and held it out to him. "Take this and keep it with you at all times." As he slid his arm through the handle, and the gravity of our situation sunk in, I was overwhelmed with emotion. A single tear ran down my cheek. "Promise that you'll come back to me."

He wiped the tear away with his thumb and leaned down. His face was only inches from mine. "There's nothing in this world that could keep me from you."

"Say the words," I insisted as my eyes swam with tears.

"Kalin." He rested his forehead against mine, closing his eyes. "You are my home. I will always come back to you."

Rowan pressed his lips against mine, and I kissed him with all the passion I could muster. I wasn't sure how much time passed before he pulled away. However long, it wasn't enough. Before I had time to catch my breath, we stood in front of a fire court portal. The ring of fire wildly swirled as we latched onto each other one last time. I held my breath as he strolled toward the pathway. He was already inside when he glanced over his shoulder at me.

"I love you," he said. "I always have."

I opened my mouth to respond, but he was already gone.

CHAPTER FIVE

MARCUS

"What should I do with her?" the hound asked.

We stood inside the fire court castle in front of Selene's old bedroom. It wasn't what I'd consider a bedroom. At one time, it was more like a small luxury apartment. But since she'd left with her brother, her quarters had been looted by hounds that were once forced to serve her. "Leave her with me," I answered.

"Are you sure?" he asked, watching her as she squirmed in her shackles. "She could be dangerous."

He wasn't wrong. Selene was a banshee. If she were fully trained, she could destroy us all with one shrieking scream. But she was more princess than a warrior. Prisma always doted on her, dressing her in lavish gowns and jewelry that had to be worth millions in the mortal world. Her beauty was legendary. Every fire elemental in the court would've given his entire fortune to win her hand. Suitor after suitor had come to the castle, and every one of them received a rejection. No one ever knew why, but I knew.

Selene was another pawn in Prisma's game.

I opened the door to her room. "Let the other hounds

know we've arrived. Have the kitchen prepare a feast." I put my hand on his shoulder. "We're all going to need our strength for what's to come."

Reluctantly, they released her. She pulled her arms away in a show of defiance. That made me chuckle. As the other hounds made their way down the dark hallway, they periodically peered over their shoulders to check on us. They were much more concerned than I was, but I'd known Selene for a long time. She was smart enough to know she needed protection after she betrayed her twin brother. There was zero chance she planned to run away. As much as I was sure she hated her circumstances, we were all she had left.

I motioned for her to step inside her bedroom. "Ladies first."

Raising her chin, she did as I asked. I followed behind her. We both gasped. It was worse than I'd anticipated. Furniture lay in burned, scattered pieces. All the bed linens and curtains were gone. The deep wood canopy was still intact, but the mattresses had been sliced and diced. Wallpaper was ripped, hanging off the walls in clumps. The closet doors were missing, as were all her expensive clothing and jewelry. This burglary was more than a simple robbery. It was clear that whoever had done this hadn't liked her very much.

"I suppose you're enjoying this," she said, turning away from me as she tried to hide her reaction. But she was too late. I saw the tears welling in her eyes.

I took the iron key out of my pocket and removed the shackles on her arms and legs. "If you're implying I find joy in your pain, you're wrong."

"It's what I deserve, right?" she said, rubbing her bruised wrists. "To suffer for what I did."

I raised an eyebrow. "Is that what you think?"

"Why are you releasing me?" she asked, avoiding my question.

"I'm not a big fan of imprisonment." I set a chair upright that had fallen on its side. "Plus, I know you're not going anywhere."

"You're sure about that?" she challenged, narrowing her eyes. "Don't forget what Orion said. My return could all be part of Valac's trap."

I closed the distance between us, and she flinched as if she expected me to strike her. Only victims of physical assault reacted that way. A lump swelled in my throat. Stepping back, I put my hands up in retreat, so she knew that wasn't my intention. "You don't have to fear me, Selene. As long as I am here, no harm will come to you."

She remained silent as if she were deciding whether or not to believe me. After several long moments, she softly replied, "I understand."

It took me a minute to wrap my head around what had happened. That reaction wasn't what I was expecting from her. All the assumptions I'd made about her over the years faded away in an instant. As she stood in the center of the room, idly rubbing her hands up and down her thin pale arms, she looked so fragile. It was like I was watching a baby bird that had fallen from its nest.

Alone, helpless, and broken.

I stared at her torn dress. "Let's find you something else to wear. I doubt it will be anything like what you wore in Prisma's court, but it will be better than what you have on."

"Why are you treating me with kindness?" she asked, voice filled with confusion. "I was never friendly to your kin. I treated you like servants."

I shrugged. "You treated us like servants because we were your servants."

"I wasn't considerate. I could've been." She glared at the floor. "But, I wasn't."

"Look, I get why you're saying all of this, and I understand why you'd expect me to want to hurt you, but that's not who I am. It never was. So, let's keep the past in the past where it belongs." I tapped my hand over my stomach. "Besides, I'm starving. It's been like three hours since I ate anything."

She laughed, holding her hand over her mouth. "Three hours?"

"I never like to wait more than two hours between meals." My stomach growled. "It makes me cranky."

Smiling, she nodded her head.

I scoured through several rooms in search of clothing in her tiny size. Selene had a figure like a mortal ballerina. Most of the apparel I found would've fallen right off of her. Finally, I had to settle on the black uniforms the female hounds used to wear. It was a simple short-sleeved button-down shirt with matching cotton pants and black sneakers. She didn't complain. But it was obvious she was uncomfortable as she pressed her hands against the garments, attempting to remove the creases. She'd worn dresses with corsets for most of her life. In all the years I spent at the castle, I couldn't remember ever seeing her in a pair of pants.

We made our way through the winding obsidian hallways and down several staircases before we reached the mess hall. It probably had some formal name, but I didn't know it. That's where all the hounds in the castle ate. We were always kept separate from everyone else. Not worthy of sitting with the rest of the court. And certainly not with the elementals we were assigned to protect. The food was the one thing we had that was equal. Hounds had to keep up their strength, especially the guardians. We could eat our fill of the highest quality meats, vegetables, and whatever else we desired. Naturally, we ate until we were about to explode.

I paused when I heard the hounds chattering from the other end of the hall. Laughter, the clang of silverware, and the sound of shattering ceramic filled the air. It was normal for me, but Selene was another story. I doubted she'd ever been in this part of the castle. Why would she? This area was exclusive to the hounds. As we got closer, she tucked her arm into mine. I tensed. She had never touched me before. I doubted she wanted to, but her fear had left her no choice. She was about to step into a room with creatures that despised her family. And although she'd never caused any of us harm, she wasn't an innocent bystander. As she'd admitted upstairs, I was sure there were many instances where she could've shown compassion and chose not to.

The loud noise silenced within seconds of us entering the mess hall. Utensils were placed back down as we passed by the rows of metal tables and bench seats. Every set of eyes stared at her. She was holding on to me so tightly that I wondered if she was squeezing the blood out of my arm. I put my hand on top of hers in an attempt to calm her down. Whispers and low growls filled the rectangular space.

Slavo, one of the oldest hounds, stood up. He had once been a guardian to a high-ranking fire elemental who beat him regularly. He wasn't ever able to fight back. The scar that sliced through his cheek and into his mouth proved how brutal the situation was for him. My jaw clenched. Out of all the hounds, he hated the royal family the most. He laughed, and I nearly fell over from shock. "Marcus captured Princess Selene. And look at what she's wearing. He put her in servant clothes."

Other hounds joined him by laughing and pointing at her. Another shouted, "Make her scrub the floors with a toothbrush." Another added, "Make her clean the bathrooms."

I had to put an end to this. "Selene has betrayed her brother. She risked her life to bring us crucial information." I made a point to glare at each one of them. "She is my guest, and I expect you to treat her as such."

"But she treated us like slaves," Slavo replied. "She should be put in one of the cells with the other prisoners."

The other hounds cheered in support. They shouted out to Selene, threatening her.

"Prisma made us slaves, and Selene is not Prisma. She had no control over her own life, much less ours." I lowered the tone of my voice. "Unless you'd like to challenge me, you *will* follow my order. Do you understand?"

"Yes, Marcus," Slavo replied reluctantly.

I sat Selene next to me at the head of the largest table. Two plates of food came out of the kitchen for us. The plates had fresh fruit, tarts, and bread. Red wine came out next. Someone in the kitchen had known what she liked to eat. Three more plates filled with meats, vegetables, and bread came out for me. As long as the portions were large, it wasn't difficult to feed me. My diet was typical of most hounds. My eyes scanned the room as I ate. I trusted them, but this was an awkward situation for everyone. I didn't want to leave myself open for any surprises.

"You didn't have to do that for me," Selene whispered. "But thank you."

"I told you that I would keep you safe, and I meant it," I said, right before spooning a huge piece of baked potato into my mouth.

Selene spent the next hour pushing her food around her plate. I ended up eating half of what they'd brought out for her. "Where will I be sleeping tonight?"

Right, I'd almost forgotten her destroyed room. Judging by the reaction from the hounds, it was probably best to keep her close to me. "You can stay in my room."

Her eyes went round.

"You'll be safest with me until I can have your quarters repaired," I said, easing her concern. Rowan had insisted I move into one of the royal suites. There was enough space for several hounds. It made me feel bad about keeping it all to myself. "I've got plenty of room." I shrugged. "Besides, I prefer to sleep on the sofa."

She shook her head. "I can't do that."

"You don't have a choice."

Glancing around, she checked to see if anyone was still watching her. Most had gone back to eating. A few cast nasty glares as they chewed their food. "What will the other hounds think?"

"If they have a problem, they can work it out with me." The hounds had an unusual way of dealing with disagreements. We usually settled our disputes with violence. After a few blows, most arguments ended up getting solved. It was barbaric, but it was our way. "It's nothing you need to worry about."

After dinner, I escorted Selene back to my quarters. "I'll talk to the females about getting you some more clothes."

"Where are you going?" she asked, nervously.

"I've called a meeting with all of the hounds," I replied, crossing my arms as I leaned against the wall. "They should all arrive within the hour. I need to update everyone with what's happened. I'll be back afterward."

Trembling, she said, "Maybe I should come with you."

"There are only so many rules I can break in one day." I chuckled. "Trust me. You'll be fine up here. No one will disturb you."

She bit her lip as she closed the door behind her.

I rubbed the back of my neck as I headed back downstairs. The meeting was in the throne room. It was the first time I'd met with my whole pack since I challenged my father for control. I'd never imagined I'd become the leader of the hounds. But my father had refused to join with Rowan, leaving me no other choice. Under my leadership, we vowed our allegiance to our new king. In return, we became equal members of the fire court. No longer servants or guardians. Our new leader had delivered on all of his promises. But he was more than my king.

In all the ways that mattered, Rowan was my brother.

He was a warrior from the start. His upbringing demanded nothing less. But there was always something more in him, something his mother never understood. Although he hid it well, from everyone except me, he had compassion for his court and wanted to help them. It was hard to believe that the youngling prince who grew up in the shadows had become the leader he was today. Rowan unified our court, healed the relationship with the hounds, and protected the akasha that might one day save us all.

But I feared his greatest challenge was yet to come. Now he wasn't fighting to save a court. He was fighting to save our world.

CHAPTER SIX

ROWAN

I had tried and failed several times to locate the Ring of Dispel.

It made no sense. The ring belonged to the ruler of the fire court. I could sense it. Feel its energy, but I couldn't pinpoint its whereabouts. I'd reached an epic level of frustration. When I concentrated, all I saw was an unending white tunnel. The longer I held onto the vision, the weaker I became. There had to be something blocking my power. And whatever it was, it had to be strong. I'd hoped that the spirits within the flames might be able to solve many of the questions I had.

Until then, I'd wait before I tried again. My power needed recharging.

The timing was ideal for returning to the fire court. The closer I got to the eternal flame, the more power surged through me. This urgency was the same I'd experienced the last time I'd come to the flame. It felt as if they knew I was coming. Almost like they were waiting for me. They were able to see what went on within the court over the centuries.

They seemed to have been watching me my whole life. I sensed the connection had something to do with my bloodline.

Once I arrived at the fire court castle, I headed toward the hidden portal that led to the eternal flame. There was no access to the caves from the surface. Within the caves, tunnels went on for miles in every direction. It was easy to get lost down here, which was why most never attempted to find the eternal flame. I was one of only a few who knew the way. As I strode through the solid rock cave tunnels, the lava covered walls thumped like a heartbeat.

I stepped on piles of ash as I made my way toward the core of the planet. The sound of crackling fire permeated all around me. None of the caves had artificial light. The flames illuminated every inch of space. The temperatures rose as I got closer to the flame. Only a fire elemental could withstand this heat. Even the gabriel hounds had difficulty breathing down here. The energy from the flames was so strong that my body radiated with raw power. I opened my wings, spreading them wide as I soaked in the strength. My body felt rejuvenated.

As I reached the end of the final tunnel, I looked upon a massive cave held up by rock pillars. The cavern was as large as a college campus and inundated with a thick layer of steam. It was like walking into a sauna. The dry heat made me thirsty. Orbs of fire shot out from an opening on the opposite side of the room. That was the entrance to the eternal flame. It was smaller than the average door, but I was able to fit inside easily. I rushed through the cavern, dodging flames as I went. The spirits weren't attacking me.

The inferno was wild and unable to be controlled, much like the essence of my court.

I stepped through the entryway. A rush of heat as hot as

the sun blew against my face. Pools of smoking red lava covered the ground. Fireballs shot up into the air like comets. There was a large flat stone in the center of the room with smaller rocks all around. I leapfrogged my way toward the surface, ducking a few times as I avoided the never-ending firestorms. The blaze couldn't burn me. But I couldn't say the same for my favorite leather jacket. A raging wall of fire rose up. Sparks of yellow and orange burning light radiated all around me.

Voices faintly whispered in my head. They only spoke to me telepathically. Each time, they repeated my name. I wondered what I was supposed to call them. I bent down on one knee. "Spirits of the eternal flame, do you have a name?"

"We are all that has come before you, young prince. The life-force of the fire court. Long ago, we were once called the First Ones."

"I came today with questions, First Ones. But I think you already know that."

"The fire elemental is known to you as Merlin remains in a state of living."

I didn't know that Merlin was a fire elemental. Throughout history, mortals had written hundreds of stories about him. They thought he was a magical wizard. It would seem that they only knew part of his story. He must've been a halfling like Kalin. If he'd survived the recent centuries, he'd remained within the protection of the mist along with all the older elementals. "What do you mean by state of living?"

"He is alive. In a state of slumber."

I got a weird vision of Sleeping Beauty in my head. "Please don't tell me he needs to be awakened with a kiss because I can promise you that's not happening."

"He was forced into slumber by your mother and the current queen of the water court, Britta."

I wasn't surprised Prisma was involved. My body tensed.

I should've guessed. I was starting to think she had her hand in pretty much every crappy thing that happened in Avalon. This information also explained why Britta left the council meeting. She probably had a premonition that involved his release. "Let me guess. Only Britta can free him."

You have the power to free him, young king. At the time of your ascension, your mothers' gifts bestowed onto you. You have much left to learn.

"Can you tell me why I can no longer sense the Ring of Dispel?"

"The ring remains in flux within a portal."

Valac had found a way to store the ring within a portal. That explained a lot. Within a portal, there were pathways to thousands of places. As long as he kept the sacred artifact inside, I could never locate him—smart move. Now I had no way of knowing when he'd come for the air court shield. The situation got even more dangerous now that he had the element of surprise. "Thank you, First Ones."

"We are always here for your council, young king. Should you ever need us."

I left the First Ones and searched for Marcus.

First, I headed for his quarters. They were empty. Next, I made my way toward the throne room following the strong hound scent. There'd been activity in here, but the room was currently vacant. The last place I looked should've been the obvious choice. When Marcus was in the castle, what was his favorite activity? Eating, of course. He ate more than anyone else I'd ever known in my life, and that included other hounds.

As I came down the hallway, I heard the bustle of activity. Roars of cheer followed by applause. Was there a performance? Was there fighting? I didn't rush to find out. Marcus had control over his pack. If there was a problem, I had no doubt he'd handle it. Instead, I took my time. Whatever was going on seemed to make them happy. They'd quieted down. Then, I heard it for myself. It was a female singer. Her voice was beautiful. She sang like she was the instrument itself.

Calm washed over me in waves.

It was familiar like I'd heard her before. Now I was curious. I hurried down to see for myself. Standing at the entrance, I froze. It was Selene. As a banshee, she had the power to destroy. But few knew they could also use their voices to heal. Mother always pushed her to train as a weapon. Valac would've relished that ability, but only the female banshees had that special power. And now, she sang to the hounds as they ate. The entire pack was here. Why was she wearing servants' clothing? Was she forced? No, she was smiling. I'd never seen her this happy. Ever.

I leaned against the frame of the entrance door, watching with amazement. She sat on top of one of the tables singing a song about lost love. Each of the gargantuan hounds was entranced. I'd never seen them so relaxed. She must've used her healing power as a means to keep them peaceful. Which explained the calming sensation I'd felt. But what surprised me more than anything else was her reaction. She'd never treated the hounds as any more than servants or guardians. Now she was entertaining them. It was the oddest thing. When she finished her song, they each stood up and applauded. Many begged for another song.

Marcus finally noticed me. I tilted my head to the side, and he followed me out. I scratched my head. "What did I walk into?"

"It's pretty shocking to me, too," he replied, looking genuinely surprised. "After we had a pack meeting, I sent for Selene. She wasn't hungry, but she came anyway. Some of the children wanted to meet her, and she mentioned she could sing." He shrugged. "You saw the rest."

I tried to appreciate what I saw, but I had my suspicions. I couldn't forget that she was Valac's sister. "Don't let your guard down, Marcus. Never forget she's played a part in all of this."

"I think there's a lot more to her than you know." He cupped his hand around my shoulder. "You should give her a chance."

"You're taking up for her?" Smiling, I shook my head. "Every time I think I can no longer be surprised, something incredible happens that changes my mind."

I spent the next several minutes explaining everything that had happened. Marcus was most excited about the shield. Like most elementals, he had no idea the sacred artifacts were real. The last few weeks had been an eye-opening experience for us all.

His eyebrows rose. "Does it increase your power?"

I hesitated, sensing what he wanted. When I was sure he was about to start salivating, I asked, "Do you want to hold it?"

"Hell yeah, I do." It was like watching a child with a new toy. Marcus slid his arm through the handles, and his whole body twitched. "Wow, this is no joke. I feel powerful, like I do after I've shifted."

I massaged the back of my neck. "It's intense."

He ran his palm across the three red bands. "And you're going to use this to defeat Valac?"

"Yup." I nodded. "Valac will come for it. It's the missing piece he needs to cut the mist."

Stepping back, he shifted into a fight stance and practiced maneuvering with it. "Don't get cocky with this, Rowan. The shield can protect you to a certain extent, but there's a lot of exposed skin. Don't forget that Valac will be stronger with Excalibur."

I hadn't forgotten. My attack had to be smart. Otherwise, there was a good chance that I'd die. "I won't underestimate him. This time I have a plan, which means I'm going to need your help."

CHAPTER SEVEN

MARCUS

"When you're ready, the pack will be by your side."

"I have no doubts, brother," Rowan replied, pulling me in for a handshake, hug combo.

"You guys look like you're about to make out," Ariel said, playfully. "I can come back later."

There she was. Ariel, the elemental I wanted to be with for the rest of my life. She was stunning in a short pale blue dress that matched her eyes. Her long wheat-blond hair hung straight down to her lower back. In my eyes, no one was ever more beautiful. I grabbed her around the waist and hoisted her in the air. "I've been waiting for you."

She hugged me around the neck. "I couldn't wait to get here. What's the big surprise?"

I put her down. "Finally, I get you both together without a looming disaster."

"Oh, I'm part of this too?" Rowan asked, crossing his arms. "I hope this isn't the intro to a threesome because I'm not sure how Kalin would feel about that."

I rolled my eyes. "You had to make it weird, didn't you?"

"What is it?" Ariel asked, with eyes rounded.

"Follow me." I intertwined our fingers and tugged her along.

I led them back to the mess hall. All of the hounds were still there with their families, listening to Selene. When we walked in, she stopped singing.

"Is that Selene?" Ariel asked, looking both shocked and excited.

"Caught me by surprise, too," Rowan replied.

Selene followed him with her eyes as we made our way into the room. She wore the same expression of terror that she'd had when I first brought her in front of the hounds. It's hard to believe that someone with such great power had so much fear. Those two had a complicated relationship like no other. Although Selene never protected Rowan as a child, she did stop Valac from killing him. She cared for him, and I believed he felt the same—even if those feelings were buried deep under some serious anger and resentment.

Every head whirled around in our direction. I inhaled deeply, then let it out slowly. I didn't want to blow the big moment. "Except for Kalin, I have everyone that means the most to me in one room." I led Ariel to the center of the space. She glanced around nervously as all eyes were on her. I reached out to hold both of her hands. "I've known you for most of my life. Our relationship is about as far from simple as any could be." Some of the hounds snickered at that. It was unheard of for a hound to be in love with an air court elemental. We mated mostly among our kind, or with the occasional mortal. "But throughout all the hardships in my life, you've been there for me. You've always believed in me and even loved me. I doubt I will ever deserve you. But by some stroke of luck, you love me back." A few of the female hounds sighed. I bent down on one knee and held out the family heirloom that had once belonged to my mother. The ring wasn't lavish. It was a simple platinum band with a round diamond in the middle. Ariel put her hand over her mouth as tears brimmed in her eyes. "I love you with all of my heart. Will you have me?"

"Yes," she began to cry, holding out her hand. I slipped the ring on her finger. "For the rest of my life. Yes."

The pack cheered as I lifted her over my head. When I released her, she reached up to kiss me. I felt her tears on my cheeks. For the first time, I was whole. The girl I'd spent most of my life dreaming about wanted to be mine forever. No matter what happened in the future, I would be okay because I had her. We had each other. It was everything I'd ever wanted, and more than I dreamed possible.

"I'm glad I got to see that." Rowan put his hand on my shoulder. "Thanks for letting me be a part of it. I only wish Kalin could've been here."

I glanced at Ariel. She stood in the middle of a group of females, showing off her ring. "I have a feeling she'll hear all about it."

He laughed. "No doubt."

I raised my eyebrows. "So, what's your answer?"

"What's the question?"

Rowan was the closest thing I had to a brother and my best friend. I wasn't sure I could ask him without choking up. "Will you be my best man?"

He pulled me into a hug. "It would be an honor."

AFTER ROWAN WENT OVER HIS PLAN, I INSISTED ON GOING with him. He rejected my offer. Valac seemed to be one step ahead of us at all times, which meant he had spies within each of the courts. He'd likely already known Rowan took the shield from the air court, and this castle would be where they searched first. For that reason, I had to remain here to lead the court if necessary. I positioned the hounds all over the castle and around every pathway. There was no chance of a surprise.

I said my goodbyes to Ariel, sending her back to the air court. If there was going to be a battle, I needed her to be as far away from it as possible. She had trained and was capable of handling herself. But she would be a distraction for me. There was no way I could fully function, knowing her life was in danger. I wasn't sure what I'd do if something happened to her. My heart ached at the thought.

I had to push those feelings aside and focus on what was happening right now. I headed over to the weapons arsenal. The room was left unlocked in case of an emergency. When I flipped on the lights, I saw hundreds of iron swords hanging on the side of the wall as well as armor piled up in various sizes. These weren't weapons for hounds. We only needed to shift into our animal form. These weapons were for the knights.

Selene surprised me when she stepped inside. "I want to help."

"Are you sure you can?" I asked, crossing my arms. "I mean, Valac's your brother."

She stood still for a moment, and then she ran her fingers over a leather glove. "I'm not saying it will be easy, but I'll do what I can to stop my brother."

"I'd prefer it if you stayed in my room." She opened her mouth to say something, but I held up my hand. "He will see you as a traitor for what you've done, and I believe he'll kill you. I'm not sure if you're capable of doing the same to him."

"Why do you care if I live or die?" She asked, her eyebrows creased. "Why do you continue to be so kind to me?"

"Because you're part of this court." I bent down, lowering my eyes, so we were level. "You have a place here."

Shaking her head, she replied, "I don't deserve it."

"Everyone deserves a second chance." The corner of my mouth quirked up. "One day, I think Rowan will see that too."

Her jaw went slack. "Not likely."

"You don't know him like I do." I pulled several swords off the wall and began stacking them on the table in front of me. "He'll come around."

She sniffled. "I owe you an apology."

"No, you don't," I replied firmly.

She wiped the tears off her cheeks with the back of her hand. "After watching you propose to Ariel, I realized what an idiot I've been. The hounds aren't animals. They're fire elementals, like me. You're my equal in every way. Maybe even better. I shouldn't have listened to my family. I should've been stronger."

I'd always thought that Selene was different from her brother. There was a kindness in her that she hid. And now that she was away from her brother's influence, she saw clearly for the first time. She was braver than she knew. "If that's how you feel, then treat today as the first day of your new life. You can be anything you want to be. And I'd be proud to call you friend."

She ran over and threw her arms around my neck. "In my whole life, I don't think I've ever had a real friend."

I wrapped my arms around her waist. "You do now."

CHAPTER EIGHT

ROWAN

There was no welcoming party when I arrived at the water court.

Britta had knights waiting only a few feet away from the portal. That premonition thing was a fun little trick to have. Unfortunately, it was power only she possessed. The knights escorted me inside the castle. As we strolled over the white sand beach, I saw all types of water elementals. Mermaids, sirens, and selkies each studied me as they sauntered by in their naked mortal forms. Once they passed through the mist that protected the water territory, they shifted into their creature forms.

I hadn't been down here much over the years. For the most part, Britta kept the members of her court in seclusion. Although they could travel all over Avalon, they remained in the water. Out of all the courts, hers was the most mysterious. Many believed they could only speak through telepathy, but I knew otherwise. During one of the rare times Prisma invited me to visit her, I overheard two water elementals speaking to one another. Their voices were soft, and they sang their words. I never told anyone about that day. I assumed Britta had a reason she kept them quiet.

The knights led me through various winding hallways filled with paintings. The entire history of the elementals was on display. Each one featured portrayals of the different creatures of her court throughout the centuries. Oddly, I noticed several portraits of a male mortal. The first paintings were of her with a mortal child. He aged in each one I passed, all the way up to the young adult years. By the style of his clothes, I'd guessed he lived around the twelfth century. It was obvious that this mortal had been very important to her.

I stood in front of the entrance to Britta's throne room. Upon entering, the scent of salt flooded my nostrils. We strode across white sand flooring. Dark green seaweed covered the walls. Steps made of large seashells led to her throne, but the actual chair she sat on reminded me of a massive salmon-colored clamshell. No one was here. Pillars made of multi-colored coral were in every corner of the room. The only thing missing was water, which was kept out by the separate magical mist that surrounded her territory like a dome.

I jolted when I heard her voice in my head. *"Why have you come, young king?"*

Turning around, I saw that she stood only a few yards behind me. Her jet-black hair was twisted into a bun and held up by starfish. Her midnight blue, floor-length gown dragged behind her several feet. The deep color of her dress against her pale skin made her look even more ethereal than usual. I bowed my head to show her respect. "Don't you already know?"

Britta smiled briefly. *"Yes."*

She already knew my intentions, so there was no point in wasting any more time. "I need you to release Merlin. He might be the only elemental who can save us."

She ambled toward the window with such elegance that it seemed as if she were floating. *"Kalin can save us."*

Yes, by sacrificing her life. That wasn't an option I was willing to accept. I shook my head. "I won't let that happen."

Britta continued to stare out the window with her arms clasped loosely behind her back. From this height, she could see for miles in every direction. *"Do you know the cause of Merlin's imprisonment?"*

"No." Prisma never told me anything, especially if it was something that could've gotten her in trouble with the high council. I wouldn't be surprised if no one knew what they'd done. Not to mention, I didn't know Merlin existed until Kalin told me.

As I turned away from the window, her eyes met mine. White nothingness replaced the color in her irises. Even the tattoos on the sides of her face were glowing. *"Eighteen years ago, you were brought here as an infant. I had foreseen your destiny. That you would be the end to us all."*

Hearing those words was like taking a bullet to the chest. Before she abruptly left the high council meeting, she mentioned the events were happening as she had previously foreseen, and the end of our world was near. The part she left out was that I was to blame. "Why me? What did I do?"

As she held out her palm, a premonition flashed in my head. It was moving pictures of skyscrapers crumbling to the ground, and mortals running for their lives. Another showed a massive tidal wave that destroyed a large island. Fires burned. Cries of pain echoed in my head. All of their anguish and fear whipped through me like a tornado. I fell to my knees with my hands over my ears and screamed.

Then it all stopped, and I heard her voice once more. *"That is our future if you prevent the akasha from sealing the mist. Once we are exposed, thousands of our kind will die within hours.*

With the elders gone, the courts will fall, and the unbalanced elements will destroy this world."

A sinking feeling burned in the pit of my stomach. But I refused to accept that this was the only option. There had to be another way. In every situation, there were always possibilities. I had to make the right choice. "There's still a chance Merlin can save us."

There was a pained smile when she replied, *"If he knew of any other way, he wouldn't have agreed to sacrifice your life."*

I paused as I pieced her words together in my head. "Wait. Are you saying Merlin wanted to kill me? That's why he remains imprisoned?"

"Yes," she replied firmly.

Okay, I wasn't expecting that to be her answer. All along, I thought this was about Kalin. But now it seemed I was wrong. I needed to know more because I couldn't make sense of it all. "And my mother helped you?"

She touched the side of my cheek with the tips of her fingers, and another vision flashed. This one was different than the other. It was a memory. I saw Prisma as she raced through a portal that was collapsing all around her. I sensed her rush to find me and her desperation. And then something I'd never experienced before—I felt her love for me. It was so strong that I nearly broke out into tears.

"Your mother had come to save you." She dropped her hand to her side, and the vision disappeared. *"She convinced me that she could stop you."*

This scenario wasn't possible. It was a trick to justify Prisma's actions. She would've never risked her life for me. She hated me and forced me into exile for most of my life because she never wanted me around. All the things she'd done and said over the years didn't match up to what I saw. I took a few steps backward as I waved my hand in the air. The images she'd shown me burned in my head, giving me an intense migraine. I had to ask to be sure I wasn't losing my mind. "Prisma came here to save me?"

As if she knew what was happening, she rubbed cream on my temples. My headache instantly disappeared. *Your mother was not perfect. She made many terrible mistakes during her reign. But she was not all that you believe her to be, young king. It was her love for you that brought her here. She was prepared to die to protect you.*

No, that wasn't true. She wouldn't die for me. There had to be another reason—an ulterior motive for rescuing me. I had to push those feelings aside. I couldn't deal with all of this right now. Once I cleared my head, I asked, "How did she convince you to help her?"

She hesitated.

"Please," I begged. "I need to know."

A single tear ran down her cheek. *I discovered an abandoned mortal baby, and I named him Lancelot. I wanted to raise him in Avalon as my son. However, the mist would have prevented him from aging. Prisma gave him the Ring of Dispel, which protected him from magic, and he aged as a mortal. Those were the best years of my life. Because of her kindness, I owed her a life debt. That is why I spared you.*

What Britta said seemed to tie together, but how? How was I supposed to believe any of this after the way Prisma treated me? None of this made any sense. I rubbed my hand over the back of my neck. All of this was too much. I had to get back to the reason I'd come. The mission was about saving Kalin, not my never-ending family drama. I unsheathed my sword, pointing the blade at her chest. "Where is Merlin now?"

This is where he rests. She pointed out the window to the highest tower of her castle. *He is frozen inside a casket made of the purest iron.*

That was too easy, which made me wonder. "Will you help me free Merlin?"

"No." She kept her eyes on the tower. *"I made a vow to your mother that I would never free him as long as you lived. I will uphold my oath."*

There had to be something special about that ice. Magic must protect it. Otherwise, the iron casket wouldn't be enough to hold him. The First Ones said that there was a way I could open it. I slid my sword back in its sheath to appear less threatening. "If I open it, you are still keeping your promise to her. Can you tell me how?"

I silently waited as she considered my offer. After a few uncomfortable minutes, she replied, *"The sword you carry can break the ice so long as core fire coated the blade."*

When Orion gave me the blade, I'd known it was special. The metal didn't melt within the eternal flame. But could I ignite the blade with my core fire? I'd never even considered it. I bent down on one knee. "Thank you, Queen Britta."

I stood.

Before I exited the room, she said, *"Heed my warning, young king. Being a leader comes with great responsibility. We are often forced to perform our duties despite our desires."*

It crushed me to hear her words because she was right. "I don't know if I can."

"Remember the prophecy I told you long ago. Every decision you make ends with blood on your hands. You must decide if the blood you shed will be from one or all."

CHAPTER NINE

KALIN

I had to take a break.

My eyes burned. I'd been reading the akasha journals for so long that I had no idea how much time had
passed. And I wasn't getting anywhere. There'd been no
other mention of Merlin or the creation of the mist since
Rowan left for the fire court. I started to feel like I was
wasting my time on a dead end. Leaning on my elbow, I
rubbed my palm over my forehead. As frustrating as this had
been, I still believed the answers were somewhere in these
books. All I had to do was find them.

I flipped to the next page.

As I read the first paragraph, I straightened my back.
There was a way I could contact the deceased akasha's.
According to this journal, there were seven planes of existence. All living creatures inhabited the physical plane until
we died. The astral plane was our subconscious—filled with
every emotion that we each experience within our lifetime—
a place where all of our memories were stored. I had the
power to access that realm and also communicate. I raced
through the next few chapters, making notes as I went.

I had to go to Avalon's nexus. The center point of the isle where all four courts converged. That's where I'd find the akasha temple. The hidden, sacred place was a mystery even to the royal families. My power was strongest there. My heart swelled with hope. This book may contain the answers I desperately needed. I closed the pages, slid the journal inside my leather satchel, and headed out of the library. I questioned whether or not I should tell anyone where I was going.

No.

They might've thought it was too dangerous for me to go alone. There wasn't any time for second guesses. Rowan had been risking his life to try to find a solution, and I couldn't do any less than that. Time to create a portal. Collecting core energy into my fingertips, I made a circle with my hands. I increased the size until it was large enough to walk through. I made my way inside, focusing on the central nexus point of Avalon. I kept going until I saw a patch of grass in the distance.

I stepped out and took in the scenery. I saw the three land territories with streams of water running in between them. This location had to be it. I'd transported myself exactly where I'd wanted to go. It was my most precise portal to date. I hoped that meant I was becoming stronger or even getting a better handle on my abilities. Excitement grew in my belly, and I made a weird, giddy kind of noise. I set the leather bag down and fished out the journal. Now I had to make the akasha temple appear.

The directions said I needed a blade, which I pulled out of my back pocket. The book said I had to cut myself and let a drop of blood fall on each of the territories. Was my blood the secret to everything in Avalon? I shrugged away the question. I had to focus. I opened the switchblade and sliced open the tip of my index finger. I winced at the pain. As the blood dripped down my finger, I held it over the three land territories and then let a droplet fall in the water stream. There was an earthquake-type rumble. I trembled. Worried I'd done something wrong, I grabbed the book and ran. After I'd distanced myself, I spun back around.

Nothing happened.

My spirit sank. Had the temple been destroyed? The quake was meant to stir something. I made my way back to the nexus. I stood close to the central point, searching for anything out of the ordinary. Everything was the same, but the area felt colder. When I held my hand over the nexus, part of my arm disappeared. I screamed. When I pulled back, I looked down, and my hand was still there. Intact. Curious, I repeated what I'd previously done, and my hand was gone once more. Okay, something was definitely in there. I took a deep breath and stepped inside.

I gasped.

Beneath the hidden veil, a three-story structure stood that appeared more like a fortress than a temple. Polished silver bricks covered the exterior. It was unlike anything I'd ever seen before. Against the sunlight, the temple gave off a multi-colored hue. It was like I was looking into a prism. I counted one entrance along with twelve windows, all on the higher floors. There was an inscription in the large archway above the door. The words were in the same language as the journals. The inscription read, 'I am the unknowable force. The fifth element,'. There are five elements, not four? I was part of a separate element.

I slung my bag over my shoulder, heading toward the entryway.

As I hurried through the doorway, a rush of power whipped through me. I stopped, dropping my bag on the glimmering silver floor. My skin pulsated with energy. All my strength returned as the world around me came alive. I closed my eyes and felt the wind blowing through the wings of a bird from miles away. I experienced the sensation as if it were happening to me. A single worm was digging into the earth, pieces of soil rubbing against my body. Dolphins leaped out of the water on the other side of the planet. The waves splashed against my skin. As a child warmed beside a bonfire, my hands warmed.

They were all connected to me.

It was like the whole world was inside of me. For the first time, I understood what it meant to be the akasha. I could balance the elements with these abilities, but more importantly, I was the protector that the world needed. I opened my eyes, excited to see what else I'd find in this temple. Gazing up at the ceiling, I admired the massive stained-glass windows. Each one represented a specific court. The red-stained glass had a symbol of three balls of fire. A blue pane had three waves representing the water court. Green glass with a large tree was meant to symbolize the woodland, and of course, the air court had a yellow pane with winds that formed a circle. Above them all, there was a much larger silver-stained window with all four court symbols. No doubt, this was meant to embody the akasha.

I made my way up a set of steps that seemed to sparkle in the light, entering a room that was the length of the temple. My eyes widened. Venetian-styled mirrors floated around the space a few inches off the ground. Each one was taller than me. I had to move in between them as they shifted around. I had no idea why, but I got the sense that they were alive somehow. Mirrors didn't float. Then again, who knew what was normal in this place? I took a glimpse into each one that glided by. They only showed my reflection. When I stood still, I noticed one had broken away from the group and motioned toward me.

"Are you going to show me something?" I asked.

I'd officially lost my mind. I was trying to communicate with a mirror. To no one's surprise, there was no response—zero noise of any kind. Once the mirror was right in front of me, I stared at something as it materialized. Two forms came into view, and my eyebrows rose. It was Marcus and Ariel. Was the mirror showing me things that were happening right now? I put my hands over my mouth when Marcus bent down and held out a ring. He proposed to her. Before I could see her response, the image clouded.

"No, no, no," I said aloud when it was gone. I couldn't help feeling disappointed. I wanted to see what else happened.

Another picture came into view. It was Rowan, but he wasn't in the fire court. He was with Britta in her castle on the ocean floor. What was he doing there? I touched the mirror, and I heard everything that she'd told him. My heart sank. Merlin couldn't help us if Valac cut the mist. But Rowan refused to believe that the situation was hopeless. He planned to free Merlin even though he'd tried to sacrifice him as an infant. Was Rowan in danger? Would Merlin try to kill him again? There was nothing I could do from here. I wasn't even sure if this was a current image or something that had already happened.

"Let me help him," I screamed. "Show me how."

"You can save them all," a soft, female voice replied.

I worked my way through the room, but couldn't find anyone else. "Who are you?" I asked as I searched the enormous space.

"We are what was, what is, and all that will come to be," the voice echoed.

Out of breath from running around, I asked, "Are you here with me?"

On the opposite side of the room, I discovered a hanging mirror. It was the largest one in here, taking up most of the wall. The voice was coming from within the mirror. "We are always with you."

I'd found what I was looking for, and relief spilled over me. "You must be one of the akasha."

My reflection faded. Something else took its place. I stared at a glowing ball of light that appeared within the mirror. The voice said, "When you require guidance, you will always find us here."

Now it all made sense. The books weren't meant to teach me everything. They were meant to get me here. I was able to get all my answers directly from the spirits of the former akasha. "Can you tell me how to stop Valac?"

"Your blood is the key," she answered.

Did she mean that there was no way for us to stop Valac? That my death was the only answer? I lowered my head and let out an exaggerated breath. "Is there any other way?"

The swirling orb of light changed colors as she spoke. "This is the way of the akasha. Everything in life must balance. Light and dark. Life and death. Power and sacrifice."

The truth of her words burned into my soul like a hot iron.

The cost of this great power was my ultimate sacrifice. My surrender would ensure that the world continued. This end was my destiny. My confidence and optimism deflated like a balloon. In my heart, I'd lost a battle I was never meant to win. Although my chest ached at the thought, some part of me had known all along. I'd tried to push those feelings aside, but I couldn't. This sacrifice was certain, my purpose, and the reason I was born.

"I understand," I told the voice. "I know what I must do."

I RETURNED TO THE AIR COURT CASTLE BEFORE ANYONE HAD

realized I was gone. As I made my way through the winding halls, I sensed my time was running out. I wanted to memorize everything that I saw. Every nook and crevice, in case it was the last I'd see any of it. In all the months I'd been in Avalon, I'd barely ever stopped long enough to appreciate its beauty. Everything had always moved so fast. We'd solve one problem only to discover we had three more. It was a never-ending cycle.

And now it was coming to an end.

"Kalin, I've been looking all over for you," Ariel yelled. She held her hand to her chest as she seemed to float toward me. I'd never seen her so happy.

I forced a smile. "What's going on?"

She leaned forward, displaying the ring Marcus had given her. I pretended to be excited. There was no way to explain that I'd already watched him propose without discussing the akasha temple. The ones before me had done a great deal to keep its existence a secret, and I would do the same. "Is that what I think it is?" I asked, matching her elation.

Her eyes warmed as if she were reliving the moment in her head as she spoke. "I still can't believe it happened. I wasn't expecting him to propose."

"I'm so happy for you both," I replied, genuinely.

I listened as she went through every detail of the proposal. She'd said that Rowan was there. I hadn't seen him in the mirror, but I was glad he was a witness. Marcus had probably planned it that way. Those two were the best of friends. I hadn't known anyone that had been through more and still managed to remain as close as they were. It was a comfort to know that Rowan would have him to lean on once I was gone.

I jolted out of my thoughts when Ariel let out a dreamy sigh. "I know we've only known each other for a few months, but I want you to be my maid of honor."

"Yes, I'd be honored," I replied with eagerness in my tone.

Her expression grew serious. "Once we deal with Valac, we'll start planning the wedding."

My stomach sunk. I'd be dead by then, but I couldn't tell Ariel. I wouldn't ruin the best moment of her life. Did that mean I had to miss my best friend's wedding? No, I wouldn't. I wanted to be part of their big day. I wanted to watch her stroll down the aisle. I wanted to see Marcus's face as she strode toward him in a gorgeous dress. I wanted to witness them saying their vows. To see all my friends enjoying life one last time. Their happiness made my sacrifice worth it. "I don't want you to wait." I grabbed her hands. "Let's make your wedding into the greatest celebration any elemental has ever seen."

Her eyes widened with surprise. "Won't that be dangerous?"

She was always thinking about everyone else before herself. "Your wedding will be perfect," I assured her.

"I don't know, Kalin." She bit her bottom lip. "I thought we'd do something small."

Ariel had spent a lifetime making other people happy. She'd even gotten close to marrying someone she wasn't in love with, to elevate her parents' position in the court. Not to mention everything she'd done for me. Without her, I would've never survived. The debts I owed her were endless. It was about time something wonderful happened to her. "I want to do this for you and Marcus. After everything you've been through, you deserve the most lavish wedding of all time, and I can make that happen. It would mean so much to me."

She must've seen the desperation in me. "If it means that much to you, then let's do it."

I pulled her into the tightest hug. "Give me twenty-four hours, and I'll give you a wedding fit for a queen."

CHAPTER TEN

ROWAN

I was about to free someone that had once tried to kill me.

Not exactly what I expected to hear when I set out to find Merlin. Although I'd anticipated there would be an interesting story tied to his incarceration. Britta had risked a great deal by imprisoning him here and hiding his whereabouts. Merlin created the mist. That meant he was very powerful. Maybe even a member of the high council. His disappearance would've been noticed by many. They'd likely gone to many extremes to keep their secret buried.

And I was supposed to believe it was all to save my life.

The images projected into my mind were convincing, but I still wasn't fully sold on the picture Britta painted of Prisma. I'd spent too many years being ignored to accept that beneath all of her anger and resentment, she loved me. If she'd feared I would destroy the world, I figured she would have told me. That was pretty important information to keep hidden. The most logical move would've been to keep me close to her. Not send me to Kalin, knowing I would eventually fall in love with her and do anything to keep her safe.

Although Britta made it seem as if we couldn't stop Valac from cutting the mist, I hadn't lost hope. Merlin was still our best chance to save Kalin. Would he try to kill me the minute after I freed him? Maybe. There was no way to know what he thought after all of these years. The confinement could've driven him crazy. What if he'd been awake the entire time? Being frozen for eighteen years in an iron box doesn't sound like anything I'd ever want to experience. I shivered just thinking about it.

Regardless of the danger to myself, I had to try.

Britta had led me to the tower where he remained a prisoner. I headed up the circular stone stairwell that never seemed to end. I was sure I'd been going for at least twenty minutes before I reached the top. I stood on the cement landing staring at a worn wooden door with no handle or keyhole. I tried to ram it open with my shoulder, then kicked it as hard as I could. No luck. Britta must've left out the part of the story that explained how to get through the magically protected door. If I wasn't able to break her seal, I had one more option.

Burn it down.

I ignited my core fire in my hands, letting the fire burn to my wrists. With as much force as I could muster, I slammed my palms against the door. I held on to the wood. My power flowed out of my fingertips, reaching the central point of the timber. Smoke engulfed the stairwell as the fire crackled. Ash filled my nostrils. I sensed it was working. Any minute now. I pulled my hands back and watched the inferno burn. A crack split the center of the door. It was time. I punched my fist into the middle of the newly formed gap.

The wood broke into large pieces, and I stepped through the frame.

When the smoke cleared, I took in my surroundings. The circular room was all brick with four square windows. No designs or markings anywhere. And in the center, I saw it. The horizontal block of ice had to be eight feet long. Iron belts wrapped around it like a medieval present. The metal hummed with magic. As I approached, the sound increased. Then I felt the pressure. Something forced me back. Each step I took was harder than the last. I kept pushing forward with all of my might. By the time I reached Merlin, my muscles were sore. Between that and getting through the door, I hoped I hadn't used too much of my core strength.

I unsheathed my sword.

Concentrating, I focused all my remaining power on my sword. A blue fire ignited all around the weapon from handle to tip. It was pretty badass. Britta hadn't explained exactly how I'd free him. I expected that I needed to break those iron belts. Reaching back, I swung the blade into the iron with all my strength. The sheer ferocity of the impact caused a loud explosion. I was thrust backward, slamming into the brick wall. Bones in my spine cracked, and I winced as I hit the floor. I was sure I'd be feeling that for a couple of days. When I got to my knees first, I crawled over to Merlin.

The metal had been bent and curled outward. Ice was everywhere. I held onto a large chunk as I got to my feet. Merlin was on the floor with his eyes closed. His arms crossed over his chest. He was a lot younger than I expected. All the stories I'd heard described him as an old mortal with a long white beard. They were way off. He looked to be in his early thirties with dark brown hair and a muscular build. He wore dark pants with a long knitted matching shirt. His tattered clothes looked like he'd been in a fight before he went in there.

I freed him, but he was unconscious.

How was I supposed to get him out of here? I'd used up most of my energy. I only had enough left to steer us through a portal. That was it. There was no way around it. He had to wake up. I bent down and tried to shake him. "There's no kiss coming, Sleeping Beauty. I can promise you that."

Since Merlin was a fire elemental, there was one thing I could try. A transfer of power. I'd heard it could be done to save someone that was in a coma or completely drained. It was a myth among our court. I'd never actually heard of anyone attempting it. It was even more dangerous with my power drained. But I had no other ideas. Why not give it a go? I placed my hands over his chest. Using my power like a defibrillator, I sent a shock into his heart. His entire body jerked. I'd try one more time with all my strength. Pressing my palms against his skin, I thrust two more jolts into him.

His eyes flashed open, and he gasped for air.

I put some space between us in case he decided to attack. He sat up sharply, his eyes darting from one side of the room to the other. Was he trying to figure out where he was? His stare settled on me, and I gripped the handle of my sword. "You're in a tower in the water court."

He managed to get on his knees, but his arms wobbled. He had to be experiencing muscle atrophy. I couldn't imagine being frozen for eighteen years was good for the body. A normal mortal wouldn't have survived. But elementals were built differently. Our bodies were much more durable. "Will you take me to the eternal flame?"

The flame was likely the only way he could recharge his power. It wasn't a bad idea. I was also in need of some rejuvenation. "Can you walk?" I asked, pointing over my shoulder. "The portal is about half a mile from here."

He squinted, and I wondered if his vision hadn't fully returned. "I will manage," he replied as he steadied on his feet.

I clutched his bicep to keep him sturdy as we headed down the steps. He patted my hand like he was showing gratitude. I was surprised he hadn't asked me any questions. If I'd spent that much time imprisoned, I would've had thousands of things I'd want to ask. "My name is Rowan, in case you're wondering. I'm the king of the fire court."

He turned his head to face me. "I know who you are, Rowan. I know everything about you."

My eyebrows drew together. "How is that possible? I mean, no offense, but you've been a popsicle for eighteen years."

He chuckled, then coughed. "That's a long conversation for another time."

I wasn't sure I liked the sound of that. After a while, we reached the bottom of the stairwell and made our way outside. "It's not much farther," I said, as we strode over the sandy beach.

"I remember the way."

I wasn't sure whether or not I should trust him. Although he was in a weakened state, the eternal flame would fully revive his power. Was that the best move? I needed to know more before I took him there. "Do you remember why Britta put you in that prison?"

The corner of his lip curled. "Are you asking because you fear I might harm you?"

I almost laughed at his response. He might know who I was, but I doubted he knew much about me. "If you're planning to attack me, you'll be the one with a sword to the throat."

"I don't have any desire to hurt you, Rowan," he tried to assure me.

Really? That seemed like an odd statement to make considering what he'd tried to do the last time we were together. "If all that's true, why did you try to kill me?"

We were a few yards away from the portal. The pathway swirled with orbs of fire. It seemed to spark as we got closer as if it had seen us coming. "I feared there was no other way," he replied. "Britta told me you would fall in love with the akasha, and that you would protect her instead of our kin. I didn't want you to have to make that choice. Killing you seemed like mercy at the time."

Did he still feel that way? Was I setting myself up for a trap? I stopped and shifted in front of him. "And now?"

"You are the king of the fire court." His eyes bored into mine so intently that I shuddered. "I believe you will make the right choice."

"Isn't there any other option?" I asked, with desperation in my tone. "There has to be another way to seal the mist."

"There is not." He lowered his head. "The blood of the akasha was the fail-safe in case the mist was ever weakened or torn. At the time of its creation, I never imagined any elemental would be able to collect all four of the sacred artifacts necessary to cut the mist."

All my hopes disintegrated. "I can't believe this is happening."

"I'm sorry, Son." His hands fell to his sides.

The words he spoke triggered something in me. Something I'd wondered all of my life. A story Prisma had told me that never added up. My eyes narrowed. "Son?"

"Didn't anyone tell you?" He asked as a line etched between his brows. When I didn't answer, he let out an exaggerated breath. "Rowan, I am your father."

CHAPTER ELEVEN

KALIN

I'd gotten in way over my head.

Trying to plan a wedding in twenty-four hours was insane. Idiotic. But I had to do it. Ariel was wild with excitement. We had every elemental in the castle involved. Everywhere I went, workers raced around me in every direction. The wedding ceremony would take place outside on the side of the mountain where Dad used to meditate. It had the best view of Avalon and happened to sit on a fairly flat surface. Ariel loved the idea. As an air elemental, she wanted to be among the clouds.

I headed outside to check out the preparations.

Wooden chairs with white silk pillows had been brought out and arranged into two rows. They had nearly finished a stage they built for the bride and groom to stand on. On either side, two white pillars stood. Garlands of fresh flowers in a riot of colors would be hung from the columns forming a floral curtain archway. Several females sat in a circle as they sewed the blossoms into long strands. Once they finished, this would be the perfect romantic backdrop. I had no doubt Ariel would love it.

Pleased by the progress, I made my way toward the ballroom where the elementals version of reception would take place. It made sense. There would be a lot of space for dancing as well as tables for eating and conversation. I stepped inside. Preparations had already begun. White round tables lined every corner of the room. Each had lavender silk draped over the surface. Purple was Ariel's favorite color, and I wanted to make sure it was everywhere. Each table had white ceramic dinnerware, champagne flutes, and silk napkins. The centerpiece was a bouquet of lavender roses that had been shaped into a large round ball and set inside a glass vase. Above my head, tiny balls of light illuminated the room like stars. The ceiling was breathtaking, and I couldn't stop the girlish shriek that escaped my throat.

Before I checked on Ariel, I needed to peek in on the kitchen staff. I let my nose lead the way as I sauntered across the ballroom floor. I approached the entrance to the kitchen. Cinnamon and sugar wafted into my nostrils. I pushed against the swinging doors and stepped inside. At least twenty elementals were moving around the area. A few stood in front of the ovens as they appeared to be waiting for food to come out. Others worked feverishly, mixing ingredients in bowls. In the far corner of the room, I saw the beginning of a wedding cake. So far, they'd made the cake layers and stacked them on top of one another. It looked like vanilla, but I wasn't sure. I didn't want to ask because everyone was so busy.

I left without saying a word to anyone. Upstairs, Ariel was in her room. She had dressmakers running in and out of her quarters for the last few hours. It had been a while since I'd seen her. I headed up several flights of stairs. As I made my way down the hallway, I thought about Marcus and Ariel. They'd fought so hard for their relationship. From the start, it was troubled. Marcus was still learning to control his new hound form when they met. He was in constant pain as his body got used to the shifting required during the transformation. It wasn't an easy process.

But his time with Ariel seemed to ease the hurt. She'd told me she quickly fell in love with him, but he pushed her away. He'd known that air elementals typically mated with others of our kind. Not to mention, her long-standing betrothal to a high-ranking air elemental. The last thing her parents wanted was to see her with a hound—the one-time servants of the fire court. Marcus thought he was doing the best thing for her. He was wrong. Ariel deserved to be with someone she loved. Eventually, she convinced him. And now, two of my favorite elementals were going to get to spend the rest of their lives together.

Their love was worth the sacrifice I had to make.

I knocked on her door and then turned the knob. I put my hand over my mouth as tears welled in my eyes. Ariel looked like something out of a fairy tale. Her long, wheat-blond hair hung loosely down her back with small white flowers weaved into the curls. Her makeup had been applied using natural tones and glossy pink lipstick. She wore a satin one-shoulder wedding gown with a pleated wrap bodice, multi-tiered skirt, and ruffled six-foot train. The purple dye in an ombre style lined the rim of her white dress. The dressmakers worked all around her, sewing all the final touches.

Ariel noticed that I stood at the door, and her smile lit the room. "What do you think?" she asked, grinning from ear to ear.

"You're gorgeous," I replied. "Like something out of a dream."

"It feels like a dream," she gushed. "I can't believe it's finally happening."

"Oh, it's happening." I thought about the workers and all

that everyone had accomplished thus far. "You should see what they've done downstairs. It's amazing."

Her eyes rounded with excitement. "I'm going to wait until the wedding. I want to see it for the first time when I walk down the aisle."

That made sense. If it were me, I'd probably want to wait too. "I promise you'll love it."

Placing her hand over her heart, she said, "I can't thank you enough for all you've done."

"Are you kidding? I should be the one thanking you." I made my way over to her. She stood on a block of wood that made her a foot taller than me. "I would've never survived without you. You've been my protector and best friend through all of this."

"I could say the same to you. Without you, I'd be forced to marry someone I'd never love." She motioned her hand around the room. "You made all this possible."

I'd told her that she shouldn't let her parents make such an important decision for her. I even offered to give a royal order, which demanded she marry Marcus. Her parents couldn't intervene in that case. But she took care of the matter on her own. "I convinced you to fight for what you wanted. The rest was all you."

"I love you so much." She bent down and hugged me around the shoulders. "You know that, right?"

Tears welled in my eyes. "Okay, we'd better stop before you ruin your makeup."

Sniffling, she released me and dabbed the bottom of her eyes with the tips of her index fingers. "Yeah, I am looking pretty hot."

I laughed. "The hottest."

She nudged me. "Speaking of hotness, it's about time we get you ready."

I glanced down at my black tank top and cutoff jean

shorts. "I'm going to have to agree with you. This outfit isn't screaming 'formal wear.'"

"I have a surprise for you." Ariel bit her lip.

I grinned. "What kind of surprise?"

"Turn around." She pointed toward the left corner of the room.

I did as she asked. That's when I saw it. Two seamstresses held up a floor-length lavender gown. Insanely gorgeous didn't begin to describe this dress. It was a strapless mermaid-style with a heart-shaped neckline and tiny lace short sleeves that draped over the shoulders. When they flipped the dress over, the same lace covered the entire back. It looked like I'd be going braless in this garment. That wouldn't be a problem since I didn't require much support in that department.

"It's perfect," I gushed.

"Why don't you try it on?" she asked, waving the seamstresses over. "I gave them your measurements, but you never know."

They handed me the dress, and I went inside her bathroom. It wasn't as large as mine. The design was pretty simple. The white porcelain sink, toilet, and tiles of the same color lined the walls and flooring. I slipped on the gown. Once it was pulled up, I clasped the back together and rejoined the group. I was only a few steps into the room when someone came behind me and zipped the back.

"You look gorgeous, Kalin," she called out. "How does it fit?"

I rubbed my hand over the silky skirt. "Feels good to me."

"Good." She pointed to her silver vanity mirror and chair. "Why don't you sit down and I'll get started on your hair and makeup."

"No way." I put my hands on my hips. "This is your day. I can do my own."

"I've seen you do your own," she replied, raising an eyebrow. "But I want you styled in something other than a ponytail and lip gloss."

I smiled. "I resent that."

"Only because it's true."

"I swear I can," I said, laughing. "I used to do more with myself when I was in the mortal world. I even dressed up when I went to school."

She playfully rolled her eyes. "Which makes tons of sense since your boyfriend lives here."

I dismissively waved my hand as I sat down in the chair. "Rowan couldn't care less about my clothes. He'd be happy if I wore—"

"Nothing?" she suggested.

I chuckled. "You're probably right."

She removed the ponytail band, and my long fiery-red hair fell over my shoulders. I watched her in the mirror as she brushed through the wavy mess. "How are things going between you two?"

I wasn't sure. "Good, I guess?"

"You guess?" She repeated, eyebrows furrowed. "You say that like you don't know."

We haven't had much time together since I'd become the akasha. He had duties in the fire court, and I was here doing the same. The moments we had were usually short and rushed. It made me wish that we were a normal mortal couple, even if it was only for one day. "It seems like we're always getting pulled in different directions."

"I wish I could tell you it gets better, but it doesn't." As she twisted my hair into an up-do, a look of sadness fell over her face. "I've had to fight for every minute with Marcus. Our responsibilities always seem to get in the way."

I let out an exaggerated sigh. "That's exactly how I feel."

"You have to make an extra effort to make time for one

another." I gazed into the mirror, and her eyes met mine. "I know it may seem difficult considering everything that's going on, but it can happen. I promise you."

Ariel had no idea how limited my time was. If I told her what I'd planned, she'd never let me go through with it. She'd try to convince me there was another way. But I knew the reality of our situation. And the outcome. An ache formed in the pit of my chest. I wish I had more time with Rowan. I wish I had more time with all of them. Unfortunately, that wasn't meant to be. "Do you have any suggestions?"

She smiled like she'd come up with an idea. "My wedding."

I shook my head. "Do you think I'd miss your wedding?"

"No, of course not." She chuckled, as she added pins into my hair to hold the strands in place. "But you could skip out early during the reception. Maybe you could take Rowan somewhere quiet. Somewhere clothing optional."

It didn't take a genius to figure out what she was implying. "We haven't reached the optional clothing portion of our relationship."

Bending down, she put her arms around my neck. "Is that something you want?"

Under different circumstances, we would've dated for years before I was ready. But I didn't have much time left. And I wanted to experience that intimacy with Rowan. I wanted him to be the one that took my virginity. I wanted him to know me in that way, even if it only happened once. "I do."

"Okay, then." She spun my chair around. "Why don't you let me help you plan something? Tomorrow night can be a special night for both of us."

CHAPTER TWELVE

ROWAN

"You can't be my father."

I shook my head in total disbelief. It was impossible. Merlin was a famous elemental known throughout the mortal world in books and mythology. No one had ever mentioned he had children. Not once. A baby doesn't go unnoticed in Avalon, especially if a queen was involved. News like that would've been announced and celebrated. Everyone would've known. I was sure someone would've told me at some point.

Secrets never stayed hidden for long.

He crossed his arms. "Aren't you wondering why Prisma never killed me? It would've been a lot easier than keeping me locked away."

Before I took in what he'd said, he strode inside the portal. My mouth hung open. He couldn't walk away. Not after that life-altering reveal. As I let out an aggravated growl, I rushed in after him. When I reached the other end of the pathway, he waited for me with a smug expression on his face.

It was time I put an end to this.

"She said my father raped her." I paused to scrutinize his reaction. The corner of his lip curled into a half-smile. Not expecting an amused response, I continued. "She said she killed him."

"Is that what she said?" he chuckled. "Think about it, Rowan. Prisma was one of the first elementals. More powerful than any other I'd ever known. Do you think she was overpowered and forced into sex against her will? Come on."

His words were like a slap in the face.

I don't know why I'd never questioned it before. He made sense. I'd never seen mother challenged, much less overpowered. My shoulders slumped, dropping my hands to my sides. I'd always known Prisma had a talent for lying, but I'd never imagined she'd make up a story like that. I thought even she had limitations. Once again, I was proven wrong. "Are you saying you two had a secret relationship?"

Merlin stared at the volcano about a half-mile away. The ash-covered land all around us was flat and lifeless. Not a shred of greenery for miles. Only burnt trees with no leaves and broken branches. He stood in one place, breathing deeply. The eternal flame had begun to recharge his power, and the energy moved through my body as well. Sore muscles regained their strength. And power surged from my core once more. I stretched out my wings, letting the warm breeze flow through my black feathers.

"We had no other choice," he finally said, as he headed toward the hidden castle. "Prisma was expected to marry a high-born or someone with royal blood. My mother was a mortal seduced by an incubus, which makes me a cambion. Certainly not a fitting match for a queen."

"How can that be true?" I replied, still not sure if I believed him. "Prisma hated halflings."

By the time we neared the castle, I could physically see his regeneration. As he made his way forward, his strides were longer with more power behind them. "Halflings weren't popular in any court. Prisma went along with it for appearances. If she'd been honest about her feelings, others might've suspected our relationship had gone beyond friendship."

I could barely comprehend what he was saying. Was I actually speaking to my biological father? After all these years of believing he was dead, the moment seemed unreal. My head swam with a list of questions. Trying not to show how engrossed I'd been, I kept my tone at a relaxed level. "What was your position in the court?"

"I was a healer," he replied, glancing over at me. "That's why the mortals thought I was a wizard."

I scrutinized his answers with more questions. "You never corrected them?"

He let out a harsh breath. "What could I say without revealing our kind?"

I snickered.

"What?"

"Sorry." I wasn't trying to be rude. Everything that he'd said seemed impossible. It was so foreign to me. It was like he was talking about someone else. I dug my hands into the pockets of my jeans. "It's hard for me to imagine anyone would want to be in a romantic relationship with Prisma."

He stopped and pivoted. "She was much more than you remember."

"That's what Britta said, but honestly, it's hard to believe." I raised an eyebrow. "I have vivid memories of her as a dark and merciless queen. Nothing more."

"That was only one side of her," he replied, putting his hand on my shoulder. "During the centuries I was with her, she was a good queen and loved by her court."

Good and loving didn't fit into a sentence that described

Prisma. I pushed his hand off my shoulder and kept striding toward the castle. "Those aren't the stories I've heard."

He remained by my side as we walked. "Stories passed down through the generations tend to lose their credibility."

I understood better than anyone. I'd heard plenty of rumors that had spread about me. Most had to do with the circumstances surrounding Prisma's death, and why I'd refused the throne. Few had been there to witness what truly happened. But there were hundreds of versions of the event. "I've learned not to trust most of the members of our court."

"We have an interesting collection of creatures," he added. "Some, as you know, have violent traditions. Prisma had to make difficult decisions where they were concerned. At times, she overlooked bad deeds to keep the peace. They weren't always fond of her choices. That's not the nature of this court."

The last forty-eight hours had been a roller coaster of emotions. I learned I had a father who tried to kill me and had been a prisoner in the water court since I was an infant. Prisma was a lot more complicated than I'd known. She'd even risked her life to save me. And, to top it all off, I supposedly would cause the end of the world. My life had unraveled in front of me. I stopped. "If she was all you described, what caused her to become the mother I knew?"

"After she found out about Britta's premonition, everything changed. She felt betrayed by Britta and me." He stared at the dust-covered ground. "And darkness fell over her."

The circumstances were rough, and there was a part of me that felt sympathy for her. But what she'd done since then was unjustifiable. Thousands upon thousands were hurt, or worse, by her rage. "That doesn't excuse the years of torture she inflicted."

"I'm not saying what she did was right." He paused as if he were weighing his words. "All I'm doing is trying to show things from her perspective. She'd lost everything and was left to raise you on her own. The loneliness made her bitter."

"That's the thing. She wasn't alone. I was there." My throat swelled, and I swallowed hard. No way was I going to allow myself to get emotional. "All I ever wanted was her love, and she pushed me away. Acted as if she despised me. I never once felt anything from her other than disgust."

"You were destined to destroy us all, Rowan." There was a pained expression on his face like the words hurt to say aloud. "She loved you as her son, but hated you at the same time."

This information was too much for anyone to handle. I was moments away from an explosion. Fire tipped my fingers. All I had to do was let go. "She could've tried talking to me. Maybe if I'd known this was supposed to happen, I would've had more time to find a solution."

"Prisma thought she'd found the solution when she sent you away." His forehead creased. "She assumed this was where you'd meet the akasha. No one knew Taron was hiding her away in the mortal world. When she found out, she was enraged. It killed her not to be part of your life."

"How do you know all of this?" I asked, in a higher octave than usual. "You were locked in a block of ice for eighteen years."

"I didn't have enough strength to free myself," he admitted. "But I used what little was left of my power to watch over you throughout the years."

I backed up a few steps. "That sounds creepy."

He put his palms out as if he were trying to put me at ease. "It was the only way for me to know you. I never expected to be released."

"So, what did you see?" I asked, my eyebrows creased.

"I've been with you every step of the way." He rubbed his

forearms. "It's been quite painful at times. I wish I could've intervened on so many occasions."

I lost it. "You've been with me my whole life. Really? The parent that tried to kill me as a baby."

"Rowan, I contemplated that decision for a long time." He paced around me. "I spent day after day trying to come up with an alternative. It made me sick to even consider killing you. But I couldn't let my love for you stand in the way. If someone cuts the mist, the akasha must make the sacrifice."

My hands fisted at my sides. "I won't stand by and allow Kalin to do that. You don't know her as I do. I—"

"Love her?" He smiled weakly. "I know."

Okay, he understood. Maybe now he'd help me. "If you know how I feel, find another way." The appeal came out with a tone of desperation. "Think of something that will save her life."

"I wish I could, son." He clasped his hands together like he was about to pray. "I'd give anything for that."

"I'm not your son," I replied with venom in my tone. Anger overwhelmed me, and I couldn't hold back any longer. "We might share blood, but that's it. You mean nothing to me."

"Rowan—" His voice cracked.

I held my hand up. "Forget about it. Let's get back to the castle and plan our next move."

We were silent the rest of the way as I tried to make sense of everything I'd learned. I had never felt so many emotions happening at the same time. Throughout my life, my father had walked alongside me, unable to reach out in any way. All of the times I felt abandoned, I was never alone. But what did that mean? Was I supposed to accept him as my father? Let him be part of my life?

As much as it burned, I had to bury my feelings for now and deal with the bigger issue.

He crushed my soul when he confirmed he couldn't save Kalin. I was beyond devastated. Valac had already collected three of the sacred objects. If he managed to get the shield away from me, it was all over. And he had followers everywhere, hidden in plain sight. It could've been anyone. He could've attacked at any time from anywhere. Was I going to have to stand by and watch Kalin die?

The thought made my stomach churn.

Once inside the castle, I searched for Marcus. I needed to update him on everything that had happened, plus we needed to come up with a plan to make sure Valac never got his hands on the shield. My first instinct was to go after him. Challenge him to a fight, and pray he wasn't as impossible to beat as Britta had suggested. But things had changed. I couldn't take a chance that he'd defeat me and seize the shield. If he did, that would be the end for Kalin. No matter what the circumstances were, I wouldn't let her die.

When I found Marcus, he was in the training area with at least fifty other hounds. The rectangular room had very little decoration: only cement walls, cedarwood flooring, and an assortment of punching bags that hung from the ceiling. A regulation-size boxing ring sat in the center. Each of the four corners had a padded pole and three thick red ropes that connected them. Two hounds without gloves circled each other inside.

Marcus stood on the outside next to Ethan. He was reading a letter intently, while the little blond-haired hound tried to sneak a peek over his shoulder. Ethan managed to duck a split second before he clotheslined him. That seemed to send him a signal because he ran to the opposite side of the ring and cheered for one of the hounds.

"He looks up to you," I noted, nudging his shoulder.

Marcus took his eyes off of the letter long enough to glance up at me. "He needs to learn his boundaries."

"He's young," I shrugged. "Don't you remember what I was like at his age?"

"Yeah, a pain in the ass," he replied, folding the letter and putting it in his back pocket. "Not much has changed over the years."

I chuckled. I'd never let anyone else talk to me the way he did. Most elementals were afraid to have a conversation with me as it was. But I'd known him all my life. He was my best friend and the one person I'd counted on to keep me in check. "I think I've matured quite nicely."

"Says who?" He raised an eyebrow.

I punched him in his massive bicep. He didn't respond. Since Marcus had become the leader of his pack, he'd doubled in size and strength. Any muscle magazine in the mortal world would gladly put him on their cover. He took the changes in stride, never letting his new position go to his head. He was still the most level-headed elemental I'd ever known. The best of all of us. "You could at least pretend that hurt."

Marcus noticed Merlin for the first time. He sized him up, giving him the once over. When he was satisfied, he crossed his arms over his massive chest. "I expected you to be older."

"I get that a lot," Merlin replied.

"I have so much to tell you," I said, turning their attention to me. I couldn't wait any longer. "So much has happened. I'm not sure where to begin."

Marcus tilted his head to the side, and I followed him. He led us to a private corner. "Before you do, I've got something to tell you."

My eyebrows knit together. "What?"

"I'm getting married."

"I know that." I rolled my eyes. "I was there when you proposed."

"No, I mean, I'm getting married." His eyes rounded. "Tomorrow."

"What?" I was happy for Ariel and Marcus, but a wedding was the furthest thing on my mind. We're in the middle of a war. We had so much set in motion with a new obstacle appearing every step of the way. "Now?"

"The timing isn't the best, but Ariel's excited," he shrugged. "They've been working around the clock to put everything together."

They? What was going on? "Kalin's okay with this?"

Marcus grabbed a hundred-pound punching bag off the ground with one hand like he was lifting a feather. He clipped it to a hook that hung from the ceiling. "From what I hear, it was her idea."

Now I was really confused. Why had Kalin set all of this up? Was there something she wasn't telling me? Had she already known that Merlin couldn't help us? I held onto the bag as he punched. With each blow, I slid backward several inches. If he kept going, it was only a matter of time before the bag exploded. "I'm happy for you, man. I am."

"I'm a little nervous." His final punch broke the bag. Powdered cement poured onto the floor with a hiss.

I tried to lighten the mood. "If you're worried about the wedding night, I'm happy to offer some pointers."

He let out a hearty laugh. "I've got that area covered, thanks."

"Okay, then, what's the problem?"

"It's her parents." He removed the bag from the hook and dunked it into a heavy-duty trash can. "They've never wanted her to marry me. I can't imagine they're taking the news well."

Was he going to let their opinions affect the best day of his life? "Fuck her parents."

He kicked his foot into the pile of cement. "That's how I feel, but Ariel wants them there. It's important to her."

"If they don't want to be there, it's their loss. Don't worry about it." I cupped my hand firmly on his shoulder. "The only person Ariel's going to worry about showing up is you."

His shoulders visibly relaxed. My words seemed to put him at ease. "I can't believe it's happening. I'm going to get the girl."

No one deserved happiness more than Marcus. With all the craziness going on, I was going to enjoy this moment. I smirked. "Come on, princess. It's time to get you ready for your big day."

He shook his head, smiling. "There's a good chance I may strangle you today."

"No worries, buddy." I winked. "I like to live on the edge."

CHAPTER THIRTEEN

MARCUS

Rowan didn't travel with us.

He took a hidden portal that was used by the royal family. It was the only route he was sure Valac couldn't hijack. The shield was safest that way. I invited Selene to journey with me, and she seemed genuinely surprised. As we made our way to the air court, I was still reeling from everything Rowan had told me. I would've never guessed that Merlin was his father. We'd all been led to believe that his father was dead. And all along, he was trapped in an icy prison by the two queens.

"Did you know about Prisma and Merlin?" I asked her.

"No, she'd managed to keep their relationship from me as well. But I'm not surprised she didn't tell me." She lowered her gaze to the floor. "She was always guarded."

How was that possible? I'd always assumed they were close. It seemed like Prisma was always doting on her. She kept her looking like a doll in lavish clothes and jewelry. She'd been given the best of everything her whole life. "But, you were together for centuries."

"That doesn't mean we were close. Prisma treated me like

her child," she replied sternly. "Her personal life was never part of the conversation."

After all the time they'd spent together, Prisma never saw her as an adult? Never confided in her or saw her as an equal? "That's sad."

"How did you meet Ariel?" she asked, changing the subject.

I let it go. There was no reason to keep pushing Selene. She'd been through more than I ever imagined. "I met her in the mortal world. She was fifteen at the time. She heard me when I was going through my first shift."

A confused expression fell over her face. "What do you mean she heard you?"

"The first shift is the most painful." My muscles ached at the memory. "All the bones in my body broke and then reset into different positions. I doubled in size. My skin tore as it stretched. There was blood all over the ground. It was excruciating."

She gasped and put her hands over her mouth. "That sounds awful."

He shrugged. "It got easier every time after that."

Crinkling her face, she seemed pained by the conversation. "Does it still hurt when you shift?"

"Yes." After a gabriel hound went through the first shift, we were required to return to Avalon and begin training. I was forced to shift over and over again each day until I got used to the pain. Until my body went numb, and I was near death. But all these years later, I still felt the pain. It never truly goes away. "Every time."

Her eyebrows rose. "And Ariel witnessed this?"

"She heard me screaming and tried to help. She brought me healing herbs and salve from the air court." I tried to push her away. I wasn't sure if I had control over my body, and I didn't want to take the chance that she'd get hurt. I was in and out of consciousness for hours at a time. She had stayed with me. I had visions of her rubbing the ointment into my bloody skin. But at the time, I wasn't sure she was real. The pain was so intense I had blackouts.

Selene reached out and put her hand on my shoulder as if she were trying to comfort me. "How long was the first shift?"

"Twenty-four hours if you count the recovery time." The transformation took about eight hours, but I wasn't able to move afterward. My body needed time to heal itself. I'd slept for the rest of the time. Well, I tried to sleep. Every inch of my body ached. It was nearly impossible to relax, making sleep difficult.

"You're so brave." Tears welled in her eyes. "I'm not sure I could handle something like that."

"We each have our burdens to carry," I shrugged. "Had I not gone through that, I might've never met Ariel. She was worth all of it."

"She sounds amazing," she replied, genuinely.

"I think you two would get along well. Ariel's into girly stuff like you. I'm sure you'd have a lot to talk about." She loved getting dressed up. From the gowns to the hair and makeup, she was into it all. It was odd that she'd have any interest in me. I wasn't into any of that fancy stuff. I never received an invite to any of the formal parties, but I doubt I would've gone even if I had. Those events were nothing more than a snooze fest.

Of course, I'd never tell Ariel that.

"I doubt it." Her shoulders sank in defeat. "She's friends with Queen Kalin. She probably hates me."

"Ariel's not like that," I assured her. "Neither is Kalin, for that matter. I think if they got to know you, they'd like you."

She shook her head. "Kalin will never forgive me for what I did to Rowan."

"You saved Rowan. Valac would've killed him had you not interfered." I waved my hand as if I were dismissing her concerns. "All the rest of it doesn't matter."

She smiled. "I'm really glad you invited me to your wedding."

"Really?" I raised an eyebrow. I figured she'd be bored.

"I'm happy for the two of you." She clasped her hands behind her back. "You love her, and she's lucky to have you."

"I'm the one who's lucky," I gushed.

"You've taught me so much in the short time that I've known you," she replied as her eyes met mine. "I feel like I see the world from an entirely new perspective. You are a great leader with a big heart. Trust me when I say she is lucky to have you. And I'm lucky too because I get to be your friend."

"Oh, I recognize that look." What was it with this family? First with Rowan and now his adopted sister. "This is another one of those hug-it-out moments."

With her hand over her mouth, she chuckled. "Yeah, I don't think there's any way of escaping it."

I opened my arms wide. "Come on already. Let's get this over with."

She wrapped her arms tightly around my neck. When I lifted her off the ground and spun her around, she squeaked. Her body was thin and light. It was like lifting a twig. Laughing, she replied, "All right, all right. You can let me go now."

I put her gently down. "Man, I'm really hungry. We'd better get going."

"Didn't you eat before we left?" she asked, raising an eyebrow.

My stomach growled. "That was like an hour ago."

She rolled her eyes playfully. "We'd better get you to the air court quickly before you pass out."

It took us several minutes before we reached the portal.

As we strode down the way, she wanted to know more about Ariel. I told her some stories and even threw in a few about Rowan. Her eyes fixed on me as we headed over the ash-covered ground. She kept asking for more like she was genuinely interested in learning all about us. I was glad I got to know this side of her. Once she let her guard down, she had a nice sense of humor. The easy flow of conversation reminded me of Rowan. I'd have to talk to him soon about her. They certainly had a lot of drama between them, but they needed each other—even if neither of them knew it.

The portal made of circling fire appeared in front of us. She reached out and said, "Let's go get you married."

I clasped her small hand in mine. "I'm ready."

CHAPTER FOURTEEN

ROWAN

My best friend was about to get married.

I'd always known this day would come. Marcus had been in love with Ariel for years. But the fact that it was happening today didn't sink in until I arrived in the air court. I stared up at the star-filled sky. The scent of lemongrass filled the air. It was warm for this time of night. I guessed around seventy degrees—perfect weather for an outdoor wedding. As I made my way up the hill, floating tealight candles lit the grassy path. Once I reached the top, the crystal castle came into view.

The candlelight bounced off the clear crystal bricks, giving the castle a rainbow-colored illusion. It was like something out of a dream. Pink rose petals peppered the emerald-colored grass. Chairs had been brought out and assembled into two sections. A long runner of white silk ran through the middle. I assumed the newly built stage was where they'd say their vows. I headed up the steps and ran my hand over an archway strung with a riot of fresh flowers.

"A little to the right," a voice called out.

I turned around, and my mouth fell open. Kalin stood at

the end of the aisle in a strapless lavender gown that clung to every one of her curves. The neckline was low, showing off a decent amount of cleavage. I was a fan of this dress. Her hair was in curls, pushed over her shoulder with little flowers tied in. Not too much makeup, but her lips were plum-colored. As she came toward me, her pale skin glowed in the candlelight. I froze when she settled in front of me. The strawberry scent of her shampoo wafted through my nose.

I had nothing, not even a joke or snide remark.

I was speechless.

She was that breathtaking.

"The best man stands here." She pointed to a spot a few feet away. "The bride and groom will stand right below the tip of the archway."

I still didn't respond. Instead, I tried to memorize the way she looked tonight. Every angle. Every inch. If Valac cut the mist, how would I ever let her go? How would I live without her? A sinking feeling settled in the pit of my stomach. If I didn't let her sacrifice herself, Britta's premonition would come to fruition. I'd be the elemental that caused the end of the world. But what kind of world would this be without her?

"What's wrong?" she asked.

I cleared my throat. "What do you mean?"

"You look like you're about to be sick." She ran her fingers gently down my spine. "Is everything okay?"

Now wasn't the time. Kalin had put a ton of work into the planning of the wedding. I refused to ruin this moment for her or the happy couple. I'd wait to tell her that Merlin had no other solution for us. If Valac cut the mist, it would be the end for her. And for me as well. I cupped her cheeks in my hands. A hint of pink surfaced. I pressed my lips against hers in a tender kiss. Her mouth opened slightly, and I slid my tongue inside. My hands slithered down her arms, settling around her waist. I poured every emotion I felt into that kiss.

When I pulled away, she asked, "What was that for?"

I tried to answer her honestly. "I missed you."

She paused as if she were trying to read my mind. "I know what you're thinking."

Was it possible she'd already known? The akasha powers were a mystery to most elementals. It wouldn't surprise me if she'd learned how to listen to my thoughts. Still, I chose to play it cool. "You do?"

She placed a hand on her hip. "It's the gown, right?"

I relaxed a bit. Smirking, I replied, "You are looking pretty hot."

"Pretty hot?" she coyly asked.

I held onto the small of her back and pressed her body against mine. "The hottest maid of honor in the history of weddings."

As she threw her arms around my neck, she gave me a peck on the cheek. "That's what I want to hear."

A smile tugged at my lips.

Taking my hand in hers, she led us indoors. I thought the outside was nice, but it was nothing compared to the ballroom. The second I stepped inside, the smell of vanilla and sugar surrounded me. Tiny lights covered the ceiling like a blanket of stars. Round tables lined the room with flowers arranged to look like large balls of lavender roses, and a group of tuxedoed musicians with string instruments practiced in the far corner. On the opposite end, a square-shaped tier cake with butterfly designs sat on a table draped in purple and white silk. The whole thing had to be at least four feet tall.

"Do you think Marcus will like it?" she asked. "I know it's girly overload."

Before Marcus left for the air court, he looked the

happiest I'd ever seen him. It was impossible to remove the smile cemented on his face. "If Ariel's happy, he'll love it."

"I had your tuxedo brought over." She motioned over her shoulder. "You can change in my room. Marcus is already there."

I glanced down at my clothes. "The leather pants aren't sexy?"

Rolling her eyes, she replied, "Yes, but not for a formal gathering."

"I'm not sure you can handle me in my tuxedo." I pretended to wipe something off my chest. "You might pass out from excitement or rip off my clothes. I'm hoping for the latter."

"I've seen you in a tux," she chuckled. "I can handle it, I promise."

I strode off toward her room. "You've been warned."

Finding Kalin's room wasn't difficult. That was where I slept the night of Taron's murder. But I didn't do much sleeping. I held Kalin in my arms for hours while she cried. Once she fell asleep, I tried unsuccessfully to get comfortable on the floor. She had plenty of room in her bed, but it felt disrespectful at the time. Since that day, I've snuck in a few times and managed to get a few hours of sleep with her against my chest. It didn't happen as often as I wanted. Her mother had strict rules when it came to boyfriends in the bedroom. She was fully transparent when she said no sleepovers.

But I'd never been good at following the rules.

When I reached her door, I knocked. I assumed he might be in the middle of dressing, and I had no interest in seeing mini Marcus. He answered in a white tuxedo shirt, fitted black pants, and leather dress shoes. The lavender bow tie around his neck wasn't tied. Sweat pearled his forehead.

"What's up with you?" I asked. "Did you decide to run a marathon before your wedding?"

He growled. "I've been trying to get this bowtie right for the past thirty minutes."

"That's all?" I asked chuckling. "Come here."

I held the ends of the tie, crossing one end over the other like I tied my shoes. I used my fingers to form the two bows, twisting one over the other. Then I pulled to tighten. Perfect. "How's that?"

He strode over to the floor-length mirror that hung on the wall. "This will work."

Now that we had that under control, it was time to get some answers. "Are you ready to tell me why you're nervous?"

He lowered his head with his hands fisted on his hips. "I'm worried that she's not making the right decision. I mean, the air elementals typically mate within their court." He let out an exaggerated breath. "What if her parents were right?"

"Are you kidding me?" I asked, punching him in the arm. He couldn't be serious. Didn't he know how incredible he was? He was the best elemental I'd ever known. I had more respect for him than any other. Ariel was lucky to have him. "Of course she's meant to be with you. She loves you. I've seen it. There's no one better for her than you. I don't care what court she's from."

His eyes met mine. "Thanks, man."

I circled the room. Someone had brought us a chilled bottle of champagne. I popped the cork and poured some into two flute glasses. I handed one to Marcus. "Don't forget, Kalin's crazy about me. There's something about the fire court. The ladies find us irresistible."

He shook his head, smiling. "You're ridiculous."

"That's what they keep telling me." I let out a sigh. "Ridiculously irresistible."

We both laughed.

"In all seriousness, I'm glad you're here." He held out his glass to tap against mine. "I'm not sure I could do this without you."

Our flutes made a sharp click sound when they connected. "You're my best friend, Marcus. There's no place I'd rather be."

AS INSTRUCTED, I TOOK MY POSITION TO THE RIGHT OF THE archway. Marcus stood next to me. The music began to play, and I patted him on the back. A line of air elementals wore lavender gowns in assorted styles. They strolled down the aisle with bouquets that matched the other flower arrangements. I glanced around the audience. Orion and Marlena were seated together. On the opposite side, Britta sat with several other water elementals. To my surprise, Selene was with several hounds. In the front row on the bride's side, I saw Ariel's parents and younger siblings. I let out a sigh of relief. We'd all wondered if they'd show up and support their oldest daughter. I was glad to see they made the right choice.

Kalin was the last bridesmaid to come down. She kept her eyes on me as she headed our way. She was even more beautiful than the last time I saw her. The evergreen tint in her eyes sparkled under the candlelight. She smiled the entire way, finally stopping at the opposite end of the stage. She gave me a little wave, and I winked at her. The music changed. Ariel would be strolling down the aisle any second, but I couldn't take my eyes off Kalin. Would this be the only time she'd walk down the aisle? Would I never get the chance to propose? It was unfair to both of us.

After everything we'd been through, we should get the chance to live out our lives.

When I heard Marcus gasp, I shifted my attention over to Ariel. She was already halfway down the aisle. Her wheat-blond hair hung down her back in loose curls. Little white flowers had been sewn in. She wore a white gown that was tight around the waist and fuller at the bottom. I was no expert on dresses, but it looked like the bottom had been dyed purple. The train was pretty extravagant. It had to be six feet long and was held up by flying woodland pixie faeries that smiled and waved at the crowd. I understood Marcus's reaction.

Ariel was stunning.

Marcus held out his hand, guiding her up to the stage. They held hands beneath the archway. Tears ran down her cheeks. He faced away from me so I couldn't read the expression on his face, but somehow, I sensed his joy. It was the strangest feeling. Like it was coming from inside of me, as if we had connected in some emotional way. I shrugged it off. Why it happened didn't matter. This day was theirs, and I couldn't be happier. At first, I thought the timing for this wedding was a bad idea. But as I stood by watching my best friend, I realized this was right.

After all the darkness over the last few months, we needed something to celebrate.

Ariel spoke first. "Marcus, I love you with all my heart. I'm so proud to be standing up here with you. I couldn't imagine a better person to spend the rest of my life with." She placed both of her hands over her chest. When she bent her arms forward, a glowing orb filled with her essence floated above her crossed palms. For elementals, marriage was more than a promise. Each one of us gave a piece of ourselves to our partner. It's an unbreakable bond, even in death. When she pressed the ball into Marcus's chest, he jolted.

Marcus cupped her cheek, and she leaned into his touch.

"Ariel, you saved my life the day we met, and you've been my life every day since. I never knew what love was until I found you. You changed my life and gave me a reason to live. I owe everything to you, and I still can't believe you're mine. I promise to treasure you every day of the rest of our lives." He held his hand over his chest and removed an orb of his essence. She shivered when he pushed it into her heart. I glanced over at Kalin. Tears ran down both of her cheeks. I loved her so much it hurt. I wanted to rush over and give her a piece of me. I wanted her to know me in the same way—in every way.

I broke away from my thoughts when the crowd applauded. Their kiss sealed the bond. They were now husband and wife.

Marcus turned around and hugged me. His embrace was so tight that I thought I heard a bone crack. "Easy now, buddy."

He chuckled as he released me. "Sorry."

The musicians played at a higher tempo as we made our way down the aisle. Each of the bridesmaids walked with one of the hounds that Marcus had chosen as groomsmen. When it was our turn, I held out my arm for Kalin. Marcus and Ariel would be right behind us.

I pulled a tissue out of my pocket for Kalin. She dabbed the cloth under her eyes. "Is my makeup running everywhere?"

Maybe a little. "No, you look beautiful."

"I'm so happy for Marcus and Ariel," she gushed. "I've read about the essence transfer, but I never expected it to be so beautiful."

Kalin had never witnessed an elemental wedding. She'd understood the technical aspects of the process, but seeing the event in person was something else. It's a privilege to be part of such an intimate exchange. "The commitment is much bigger than anything in the mortal world. When you accept the gift from your mate, it will stay with you for the rest of your life. You'll always sense them inside of you. I don't know what that feels like, but I'd guess it's pretty intense."

She stopped when we reached the end of the aisle. "Would I be able to do the same? I mean, because I'm a halfling."

"You're the akasha now." I tucked a loose strand of hair behind her ear. "I doubt there's anything you can't do."

The crowd had already begun to enter the reception area. As the ceremonial space emptied, I noticed that Marcus and Ariel were still on the stage. He held her in his arms while she rested her cheek against his chest. It was such a tender moment that I looked away. "Come on, Jelly Bean. Let's give them some privacy."

She glanced up at them and smiled. "I'm so glad I got to see this."

"Me too."

Grabbing my hand, she pulled me toward the ballroom. Tables were set up on the sidewall for the wedding party. We sat at the largest one, so we'd be with the bride and groom. The upbeat music played while many elementals danced in the middle of the room. Bottles of wine were the first to come out. I took two glasses from a server tray and handed one to Kalin. The flavor was a bit sweet for my taste. She seemed to enjoy it, drinking nearly half in one gulp. "You might want to take it slow until you get something to eat," I smirked.

She sat her glass on the table. "I've had enough bad experiences with wine to know you're right."

I wondered if she were thinking about that shithole, Sebastian. He'd spent weeks poisoning her with wine as he pretended to be her friend. It was perfect timing. She was under non-stop pressure to marry, while her father tried to recover. He acted like he wanted to help her. But the whole time he was weakening her power so he could seize control of the air court. I was beyond happy that he got what he deserved in the end.

"Would you like to dance?" I asked bowing.

She accepted my hand. "Definitely."

We crisscrossed our way through the dance floor crowd, settling right in the middle of the massive hall. The music dropped to a soft tempo. I slid my arms around her waist, and she wrapped hers around my neck. We swayed together to the beat of the song. I heard her let out a sweet sigh. When she pressed her body into mine, I tightened my hold on her. Our bodies fit perfectly together like we were each shaped for the other. Everyone else disappeared, and all I could hear was the sound of her breathing. As I closed my eyes, I wished this moment would never end.

A nervous rattle pulled me out of my haze. My eyes flashed open. As I scanned the room, I concentrated on this new sense of awareness. It was like a warning, and it was getting stronger by the second.

"What's wrong?" she asked, gazing up at me.

The sensation reminded me of the telepathic link I had with Britta when she spoke to me, but this wasn't just in my head. It was something I felt all over. "Something's wrong. I can feel it."

"What do you mean?" Her eyebrows knit together. "You're starting to scare me."

"I'm sorry." I didn't mean to be vague. But I had no idea what was happening. I released her from my hold and massaged my temples. "It's hard to explain. Like someone is trying to send me an alert. It's inside my head, but I can feel it everywhere."

She put her hands over mine and closed her eyes. "Let me see if I can use my power to help you."

My body jolted when she entered my mind.

"I hear it too," she said. "Let's try to move toward the sound."

I didn't have time to respond. Within seconds, we both saw what had been making all that noise. It was the Ring of Dispel. Valac had removed it from the pathway, and I could sense it once more. The ring was trying to communicate with me. I'd known the ring had a connection to the king of the fire court, but I had no idea it could contact me. I used all my energy to sense its location.

The air court mountain came into view.

Kalin stepped back, breaking our connection. "Did you see it, Rowan?"

"Alert your knights." I removed the glamour over my weapons. Some of the elementals on the dance floor screamed when the sword and shield on my back appeared seemingly out of nowhere. I released my sword from its sheath. "Valac is here."

CHAPTER FIFTEEN

MARCUS

Today was the greatest day of my life.

The musicians had already begun to play an upbeat instrumental song. We watched as our guests strolled inside for the wedding reception. Members of the royal families and high ranking elementals from every court were in attendance. It was hard for me to believe they'd all come to witness the wedding of a hound who had, until recently, been considered a step above a servant. A guardian to the elemental they once called the shadow prince—my best friend and brother.

Before we joined them inside, I wanted first to have a quiet moment with my wife. My wife, two words never sounded so sweet. I'd spent all these years wondering if I would surrender to the fierce creature I struggled to control. But Ariel was the one who made me see I was more than an animal, and that I didn't have to accept the life assigned to me. No matter the circumstances, her faith in me was unwavering. I held her tightly against my chest.

For maybe the first time, I'd truly felt the warmth of optimism.

Millions of bright stars filled the night sky. From this height, I saw little more than clouds and the edge of the forest surrounding us in every direction. A cold wind blew in from the south, and goosebumps filled the top of her forearms. "It's time to get you inside, my wife."

"Lead the way, my husband."

A scent I wasn't expecting wafted through my nostrils. I inhaled deeply. It was the familiar smell of burnt ash. There were members of my court here. But this odor was strong like hundreds of fire elementals were suddenly all around us. My muscles tensed. With one arm, I thrust Ariel behind me.

"What's wrong?" she asked, with worry laced in her tone.

I wasn't ignoring her. I had to make sure I was right before I responded. Closing my eyes, I drew in a slower breath. What I'd feared was confirmed. "A crowd of uninvited guests will be here in a matter of minutes. You have to go inside and alert everyone."

I surveyed the area around the castle. All of the royal families brought knights with them. There had to be at least two hundred. I'd been around long enough to know they'd only accept a command from their king or queen. If they weren't ready, we'd never survive the ambush.

Her eyes widened. "What are you going to do?"

Anger built inside of me. I had to hold off whatever attack was coming. The beast inside of me stirred. "Slow them down."

As she turned to leave, I held onto her wrist. "Why are you stopping me?"

I bent down, leveling our eyes. "If this is about to get as bad as I think, I need you and your family to get to safety."

She pulled her hand back. "I'm not going to abandon my friends."

"Please listen to me, Ariel," I begged, my stomach already in knots. I wanted to be angry, but her fierce loyalty was something I'd always admired. That's what made her who she was. "I can't fight them off if I think you're in danger. I'll end up getting myself killed."

Her eyelids lined with tears. "Marcus—"

My heart pounded in my ears as sweat poured down my back. A familiar sensation came over me as the change started. I reached out for her. My large hands completely covered her biceps, rattling her tiny frame. "Please promise me."

She looked away into the distance. "I—"

"Please," I repeated, trying my best to hide the pain. A fire burned in my core. Bones in my back popped as they broke. I dropped to my knees. "Promise me."

"Okay." Her voice trembled. "I promise."

Muscles tore as the bones shifted into their new position. Skin stretched to accommodate my growing size. Hair fell out in clumps, replaced by dark fur. I glanced up. Her hands covered her mouth. It had been a while since she saw me shift. It was something I preferred to do alone. As hard as it was on me, I imagined it was always more difficult to watch without being able to help. The cartilage in my nose cracked, blood dripped down my face. My snout formed. "Go," I growled.

She ran full speed toward the castle.

Not long after she was gone, the transition was complete. Now that I was in my hound form, my heightened hearing and infrared vision allowed me to see into the darkness that surrounded the castle. The thick forest was about a mile away. I hurried over and prowled the wooded entryway. The scent of ash grew more potent as each minute passed. As they drew closer, I got a whiff of elementals from the other three courts. They must've joined with Valac. It was the only way to explain the combination of smells.

A thunderous roar shook the ground.

I circled. The other hounds were coming to assist me. Knights had positioned themselves all around the castle. Each one stood with a sword and shield. They were ready for battle. Which meant Ariel had done as I asked. I hoped she'd followed all of my instructions and kept herself out of danger. I quickly brushed those feelings aside and refocused on what was happening. The ten hounds I'd traveled with appeared on either side of me, forming a large barrier around the forest.

The bulk of my pack remained within the fire court castle.

"Valac has come for the shield," I told my pack. In this form, I was able to speak to them using telepathy. Rowan had the sacred object strapped to his back. *"We must protect our king."*

"Our king has readied himself for war," Ethan replied.

That wasn't a surprise. Rowan never shied away from a battle. He certainly wouldn't start now that Kalin's life was at risk. If I had to bet, he was with her. I preferred to be protecting Ariel, but I had to stand with the pack. We were the first line of defense. As a group, we could kill most of them before they had a chance to reach the castle. I wished I'd brought more hounds with me. I should've expected an attack, but I assumed Valac wouldn't risk an all-out assault while all the courts were together.

He was more brazen than I anticipated.

I sent out a distress call, howling loud enough to shake the trees. Any members of my pack in their hound forms heard the vibration, no matter the distance. The other royal families had likely sent for backup, as well. I had no idea what to expect from Valac. My nerves remained on edge as we waited. The low growls from the other hounds echoed in my ears. When I heard the pounding of feet, I dug my claws into the grass-covered dirt and bared my teeth.

"Get ready," a voice said, shifting my attention away from the woods.

Rowan stood behind me, clutching his sword. The shield wasn't on him. He must've given it back to Kalin to protect. This place wasn't where he needed to be. I wanted him inside with her. Together, they could've defended the shield if some of the rogue elementals managed to get past us. Now, he was putting himself in danger. I wasn't able to speak to him in this form. Instead, I released a venom-filled growl that let him know exactly how I felt about his presence.

"I know you're pissed." He tried to pat my head, but I turned away. "I need to try one last time to reason with him. See if I can end this before more of us die."

His motives weren't unreasonable. Any worthy king wanted peace before war. But Valac was long past logic. He was willing to die to see this through, and I firmly believed the only resolution we'd find today would happen on the edge of a sword.

A heavy gust of wind blew through while leaves rustled and twigs snapped.

They were here.

I faced the edge of the forest. Lowering my head, I was ready to pounce the moment they charged. The rattling ground gave me the impression they planned to come in fast. One by one, Valac's rogue elementals appeared out of the brush. Each halted as soon as they saw what waited for them. Most were once members of our court. The power of the sacred artifacts likely seduced them, and whatever else Valac had promised.

There was a commotion among their ranks, and then I recognized Valac's voice. He fought his way to the front of the line to see why they'd stopped. He wore the Green Armor. Excalibur was in his hand, as well as the Ring of

Dispel. Valac spotted Rowan, and a wicked smile formed on his face. "Have you come to surrender?"

"This is your last chance." Rowan pointed the blade of his sword at his throat. "We can resolve this without any more bloodshed."

At the sight of Rowan's sword, the rogue elementals raised their weapons. Some had iron swords, knives, and axes. Others ignited a fire in their palms. The hairs on the back of my neck stood on edge. The second one of them made a move I'd lunge at their throat.

"This ends when I rule over all four courts," Valac replied, intently. "I'll return the order to Avalon and restore honor to the House of Djin."

My muscles begged to pounce on him. Valac was Prisma's adopted son. He was never a member of her house. That right belonged to Rowan alone.

"You can't restore honor," Rowan shouted, loud enough for all the rogues to hear. "You have to earn it by making self-less choices."

"I've made my choice, false king," he replied, with disdain in his tone. "Attack."

Rogue elementals swarmed us with weapons raised. Valac disappeared within the crowd. We fought against elementals we'd once considered our allies, tearing into their flesh with our teeth. Rowan was right in the middle of the violence. He slashed through any stragglers that managed to fight their way through our line. Knights from the other courts had also entered the fray. Swords clashed against one another, and I heard pained screams all around.

In no time at all, the ground was littered with bodies from both sides.

Although we'd made a dent, they had much greater numbers. A few had managed to slip past us. Rowan reposi-tioned himself closer to the castle. Any elemental that got through now had to take him on. As far as I could tell, none had reached the entrance. There were bloodstains on his sword and clothing. I was no better. Streaks of red coating stained my face, teeth, and paws. Everywhere I looked, elementals fought to the death.

No matter how many we killed, more kept coming. Bodies had already begun to decompose, converting into ash. The hounds were ferocious with their attack, taking on twenty or more at one time. I'd been stabbed a few times, though none were deep. My skin was difficult to pierce in my animal form, even with iron weapons. Immense sadness rippled through me. Out of the corner of my eye, fifty or so rogues had killed one of my young hounds. He'd taken most of them with him, but that didn't lessen the pain of his loss.

It also created a hole for them to breach.

Rowan used his power to build a wall of fire around the entire perimeter. This barrier wouldn't stop them, but it did slow the flow of elementals. The remaining hounds killed the rogues as they passed through the flames. Valac remained out of sight. Even with all the sacred objects, he let his rogues kill on his behalf. It was a smart yet sickening strategy. He'd sacrifice every one of their lives to wear us down. Once the attack weakened us, he'd likely go after the shield.

And so far, his plan seemed to be working.

Rowan wasn't going to be able to hold them off much longer. He'd dropped to his knees. I had to get him out of here. As I loaded him on my back, spinning funnels of sand flew over our heads. Each cone picked up bundles of rogues at a time and dropped them off the side of the mountain. Tornadoes plucked them off the ground like pieces of corn. They were coming in from all over. That's when I saw Orion with his hands reaching up to the skies. Other woodland elementals merged their power, strengthing the counterattack.

"You have to take me back," Rowan urged. "They'll need our help."

I ignored his request. He needed time to recharge, and he wouldn't get much of a chance this far away from the eternal flame. I pushed my way through the crowd until I found Kalin. She ran over once she realized what I was carrying.

"Are you hurt?" she asked, as panic filled her eyes.

"I used too much power," Rowan replied, weakly. He sat down on the floor. "I can still fight."

"Not like this." She cupped her hands on his cheeks. "I won't risk your life."

Orion and the other woodland elementals wouldn't be able to hold them off for long. An ache formed in my chest. Was this the end for all of us? How long would we be able to hold on?

"Help has arrived," Kalin announced to the crowd, pointing toward the window. "Look."

Streams of reinforcements from every court had joined the battle. They pushed the rogues back. I let out a sigh of relief as I glanced over at my friends. With Rowan safe, I looked for Ariel and her family. I searched the entire ballroom. She must've hidden away as I asked. Comforted that she was protected, I rejoined the other hounds. I was overjoyed to see my entire pack holding the barrier. Some of the winged fire elementals flew over the battlefield, attempting to enter the castle. Britta, along with a horde of her elementals, shot them out of the skies using her water magic.

With the blockade in place and the additional knights, we'd successfully turned the tide.

"We can't let them escape," I told the other hounds. As rogues attempted to retreat into the forest, we went after them. One by one, we chased them through the thick woodland. The ground shook as we went full speed for miles. They tried to outmaneuver us by zig-zagging through the

trees. That didn't work. We're stealthy for our enormous size. Each time, we took them down. We were ripping out their throats as they begged for mercy. We had no interest in prisoners.

They betrayed our court.

They died without honor.

As I snapped the neck of the last rogue, I heard cheers coming from the castle. The knights had claimed victory. The other hounds turned to me, and I shook my head. I had an unsettling feeling deep in my bones. This fight wasn't over. I was sure of it. *"Stay on guard,"* I told my pack.

Throughout the battle, Valac was missing. There had to be more to his plan. He'd risked too much already. I was sure he wasn't through yet. When no rogues were left standing, we made our way back through the forest. The scent of death lingered in the air. My stomach soured when I saw the battlefield. Bodies in various stages of decay peppered the area surrounding the castle. This defeat wasn't a victory. It was a massacre. Everywhere I looked, all I saw was death.

Elementals from every court searched through the carnage for their loved ones. I passed by a family that cried over the carcass of a young male air knight. The mother brushed the hair away from her son's face as tears ran down her cheeks. As I continued through the slaughter, I tried to find my friends. Marlene rushed by me in a panic. Moments later, she found Orion. He'd survived the attack, but his bloodied left arm hung limp at his side. Britta seemed to be unscathed. She blessed each of her fallen elementals as their bodies liquefied into water.

But still no sign of Valac.

Then I heard a scream that froze my blood.

CHAPTER SIXTEEN

ROWAN

I had to get out of here.

Injured elementals from every court filled the ballroom. Bodies laid on top of the tables with blood dripping down silk lavender linens onto the floor. Throughout the room, I heard pained wails. Woodland faeries raced around, mending as many as they could with the salve they'd brought. A few had been sent back to their court to retrieve more. Although they tried many times, they weren't able to help me. I exhausted my power when I created the massive fire barrier. This far away from the eternal flame, I had to heal on my own. I wasn't helpless. I still had a sword, and I could swing it.

Reinforcements had arrived from every court. It was the first time I'd ever seen all of us working together against a common enemy. They fought hard, but the battle raged on. I needed to be out there fighting, not sitting on my ass. I stared at Kalin. As she bandaged up the wounded, she watched the war from the window. She ached to be out there too. All the other leaders fought alongside their elementals. She had the power of all four elements and knew we needed her help, but she had to stay with the shield. I wasn't strong enough to defend the final sacred object if Valac found his way inside.

And as hard as it was to watch her elementals perish, she couldn't risk it.

I fought to stand, wobbling as I struggled to hold my weight. I stood on my feet for only a moment before my knees began to buckle. I let out a frustrated growl. It was useless. I had nothing left. I sat down in the closest chair, slamming my fist onto the tabletop. Heads turned in my direction, and I shooed them away. How many elementals had Valac recruited? If I had to guess, there were close to a thousand. I leaned on my elbows with my face in my hands. This ambush was my fault. As much as I wanted to see my friends happy, I should've stopped the wedding. I should've known he'd strike while we were off-guard. Why hadn't I seen it coming? At the time, the risk of an attack seemed slim. All the other raids took place during a time when the leaders were away from their courts. That left the remaining elementals outnumbered and overrun. But this assault had lost the element of surprise. We were ready and had our most powerful royal members in attendance. It was a bold move on his part and one that cost the lives of much of his force.

"Rowan, they're pushing them back," Kalin said, breaking me out of my thoughts. "Some of them are retreating into the forest. The hounds are chasing them."

The tension in my shoulders relaxed.

Marcus wouldn't stop until he killed every last one of them. We'd discussed our intentions before we left for the fire court. I had no interest in prisoners. The rogues had fought against their kin. If I had my way, none would survive the night. "Have you seen Valac?"

"No," she replied. "Not once."

He hadn't abandoned them. I still felt the presence of the

ring. If I had any strength left, I'd be able to identify his specific location. Aggravation overwhelmed me once more. This war had to end tonight. Valac couldn't be allowed to rebuild his army. We'd already endured too many losses.

"What's going on?" Ariel asked, holding handfuls of fresh bandages and ointment she retrieved from the infirmary. "Is Marcus all right?"

"They've started to retreat," I told her. "Marcus and the other hounds went after them."

Ariel handed the supplies over to a group of woodland faeries. "Does that mean we won?"

Kalin glanced over to me. Without words, we each knew what the other was thinking. This war wasn't over until Valac died. And I couldn't shake the feeling that this was all a diversion. But would he sacrifice the lives of most of his rogues to make a play for the shield? If he failed, he'd surely die. With all of our leaders in one place, there was a chance we could overpower him. The move was risky unless he had someone on the inside.

"Guard the shield, Kalin," I urged her. "Call your knights back."

My words sent out an alarm throughout the ballroom. Elementals that were able grabbed their weapons. I forced myself to stand, ignoring the weakness that threatened to collapse me to the ground. My sword felt like a five-hundred-pound weight in my hand, but I held it anyway. I refused to be helpless. Even if it cost me my life, I'd defend Kalin and the shield.

A horde of rogue elementals rushed into the room from a side door.

I was right.

They had to have someone from the air court helping them, someone who had remained hidden until now. That was the only way to explain how they'd come through the castle without anyone alerting us. Fear rippled through me. Woodland faeries raced outside to call for help, while the rest of us raised our swords. Kalin held her palm up. The wind rushed to the door, preventing the remaining invaders from coming inside. With her other hand, she pointed to a group of rogues and sucked into a large tornado-like sand storm. The same one Orion had created outside. Glass shattered as she thrust them through the window.

Mayhem broke out in every direction.

Rogue elementals from my court lit several woodland faeries on fire. Kalin propelled a stream of water at them, diminishing the flames. Then she used another tornado to eject them out the window. But she'd used too much magic in too many different directions. The rogues she'd held at the door managed to get inside. They filed in, surrounding the perimeter of the room. Screams of pain echoed all around as we fought back. One of the rogues lunged at me. I had enough strength to slice into his midsection. It wasn't enough to kill him, but at the very least, he had to be injured.

The ground shook as a hound stepped inside the room. I couldn't recognize who it was, but he wasn't on our side. Water elementals tried to force him back, but he pushed right through their attack. He leaped, crushing their chests when he landed on top of them. They were dead in an instant. Knights threw iron knives at him, which only bounced off his thick skin. I wasn't sure there was anyone here who was strong enough to stop him. Then Kalin appeared behind him, jumping on his broad back. She ignited the sword in her hand, engulfing the blade in flames, and plunged the weapon into his neck. I heard the crack as she severed his spine.

Only a few yards away, Valac stood beneath the door frame. He wore the Green Armor. Excalibur was in his hand, while the ring gleamed on his finger. His eyes locked onto her. She was so focused on the hound as she rode his back that she didn't see what was right behind her. Valac raised the sword, preparing to slice into her. Fury took over me, and I moved as fast as I could. My legs were stiff with pain, making my pace even slower. I screamed her name over and over as I tried to warn her. There was too much commotion all around us.

I'd reached the middle of the room and watched in horror as it happened.

Ariel thrust herself at Valac, blocking Kalin from his attack. The blade cut into her side, and she let out a wailing scream as she collapsed to the ground. Blood puddled around the incision, turning a section of her wedding dress crimson-red. Kalin turned around at the sound, and her eyes went wide. She crawled over to her, placing her head in her lap. The rest of the room stood still at the sight of them. Kalin wiped her hair away from Ariel's face as tears ran down her cheeks. It all happened so fast. Even Valac seemed to be stunned by what had transpired.

Only a short time ago, Ariel stood beneath a floral archway and said her vows. Now she was dying on the floor of her wedding reception.

That was when Marcus ran into the room, still in his hound form. In an instant, he was next to her. Ariel placed her blood-stained hand on his cheek. He whimpered, nuzzling his massive head into the crook of her neck. An overwhelming ache radiated from within me. But it wasn't my hurt. I sensed Marcus once more. But this time, the sensation was much stronger. I felt his grief as if it were my own. I'd never known agony like this before. It was such intense emotional anguish that it had become actual physical pain. I held my hand to my chest as his heart shattered. Then I heard his voice inside my head. *"No, Ariel. No! Please don't leave me,"* he cried. *"Not like this."*

I tried to respond telepathically. *"Marcus, I'm so sorry."*

He turned to face me. *"You can hear me?"*

"I don't know how or why, but yes," I replied, unsure how to explain what was happening between us. *"For the first time, I can."*

Marcus shifted his glare to Valac. He had remained there, only a few feet away from them, still seemingly in shock by what he'd done. *"You did this."*

He let out a roar that shook the entire room.

"Marcus, don't," I begged. *"He'll kill you."*

"Can't you see?" Marcus replied, crouching down into a fighting stance, growling from deep in his throat. *"I'm already dead."*

Valac raised his sword, ready to defend himself. The blade was still wet with Ariel's blood.

I was heading over there when Selene stepped in between Valac and Marcus, her hands straight out at her sides. My brows snapped together. Was she protecting Marcus? "Please, I'm begging you," she said to her brother. "If you have any shred of love left for me, you'll leave now."

"I didn't want to kill her," he replied, pointing his blade at Kalin. "*She* was supposed to die."

Valac went after Kalin because she was the only one that could stop him if he pierced the mist. Without her, we'd have no other choice but to surrender to his demands. Kalin carefully sat Ariel's head on the floor. When she rose to her feet, a fire burned from one hand, and a wind tunnel spun in the other. "Take your shot," she challenged, with venom in her tone.

I struggled to reach them. Giving up on my legs, I tried flying. My wings were too heavy, and I tumbled to the ground. None of us were at full strength. Even combined, I wasn't sure if we could take Valac down. "Don't do it, Kalin," I yelled. "That's what he wants."

"Please," Selene pleaded to Valac. "Let them grieve."

Marcus was a second away from pouncing, and I couldn't reach him. He was still too far away. Then it hit me. If I could communicate with him telepathically, there was a chance I'd inherited my mother's ability to control the hounds. I didn't want to do that to him. He'd experienced it before when Prisma forced him to tear off my wings. But if I didn't do something, Valac was going to kill him.

"I'm sorry, Marcus." I concentrated solely on him. Focusing on the bones in his limbs, I tightened my fists until my knuckles were white. My body was completely still. He tried to push forward and stopped mid-step. He roared as he attempted to move, but went nowhere. I'd done it. I had the power to control the hounds. *This was the last thing I wanted to do to you. But I won't let him kill you."*

"I don't care what happens to me," he snarled. *"Let me go."*

"You're my best friend, Marcus. I can't let you do this," I replied. There was movement going on all around me. I heard the sound of swords scraping against one another. But I couldn't see any of it because I needed all of my concentration focused on Marcus. He fought back. Each second that passed was harder than the last. I wasn't sure how long I could keep this up. My core force drained away at a rapid pace. If it emptied, I'd die.

"You can't hold me forever," he said, pushing back against my power.

"No, I can't," I replied, struggling to maintain him. *"But, I'll protect you until my last breath. Even if I'm protecting you from yourself."*

"I don't need your help," he growled.

There was one last thing I hadn't tried. The only way I had left to reach him. *"Marcus, Ariel is dying. There's nothing that can be done to stop it. Do you want to spend her final moments fighting Valac or by her side?"*

Instantly, he stopped, and I released him. Once the connection broke, I saw that war had exploded all around me. I couldn't see Marcus or Kalin. There was too much happening. Still, on my knees, I felt the world teetering back and forth as my vision blurred.

Then there was nothing.

CHAPTER SEVENTEEN

KALIN

My best friend was dying.

I was about to challenge Valac when I heard Marcus struggle. Something was holding him in place, preventing him from moving. I scanned the room. That's when I saw Rowan, who seemed to be in a trance. I watched it in awe. He'd told me about Prisma's power over the hounds, but he said he didn't have it. Maybe he was wrong. Neither of them said a word, so I concentrated on their bond. I caught the end of what I assumed was a conversation between them. Rowan actually spoke to him using a form of telepathy.

Whatever he said seemed to stop Marcus. I watched as he shifted back into his mortal form. Other hounds fought all around us, clearing away the remaining rogues. I spun around. Valac was gone. He must've gotten away. I reached behind for the shield. It was gone too. He'd taken it while I was trying to connect with Rowan and Marcus. How had I let this happen? Ariel had given her life to save mine. Marcus had lost the love of his life. All for nothing. Pain seared through me like a hot knife, slicing right through my heart.

Marcus took Ariel's hand. Tears welled in Marcus's eyes. I wanted to grieve with him. To show my support and tell Ariel how much I loved her. But it felt like an intrusion. They loved each other so much, and now everything had been taken away from them. It wasn't fair—none of this. Ariel groaned from the pain. The ointments we had wouldn't help her. Excalibur's blade acted as a poison. Even our strongest medicines did nothing to relieve the stress on her.

"I can't heal her," Selene said, sniffling. "But there is something I can do to ease her pain. Will you let me?"

I was supposed to be the all-powerful akasha, and yet I couldn't save my best friend. But if I could ease her pain in any way, I was willing to do it. "If it's okay with Marcus."

He nodded.

Selene bent down on the other side of Ariel. She slid her hand in hers and began to sing. Banshees were known for their screams that could kill. Not many knew they could also ease the pain of sufferers with their song. Her voice was soft and soothing. Ariel watched her as she sang, and ease came over her. Everyone around us seemed calmed. She continued for several minutes. Ariel watched her with a smile on her face. A line of blood ran out of her mouth and down her cheek.

Her eyes closed, and she took one last breath.

And then she was gone.

The song abruptly ended as Selene ran away in tears. Marcus put his head on Ariel's stomach and cried. Riddled with grief and guilt, I decided to do the one thing I could do for my best friend. I'd make sure Marcus was given privacy to grieve. I turned and walked toward a group of my knights. I pointed to them, taking one last glimpse of the greatest friend I'd ever known. A lump swelled in my throat. "I need you to form a blockade around Marcus and Ariel. I don't want them disturbed for any reason. Do you understand?"

They nodded.

The hurt from her loss made it hard to breathe.

Where was Rowan? I'd lost sight of him during the commotion. I searched through the bodies in various stages of decay, and then I saw him. He was face down in the middle of the dance floor. My chest tightened when I realized he wasn't moving at all. I raced toward him. When I reached him, I got on my knees and rolled him over. I put my head on his chest and listened for a heartbeat. Relief spilled over me when I heard him breathing. It was faint, but he was still alive. "Rowan," I cried. "Can you hear me?"

No response. He didn't appear to be injured. At least, not physically. He was passed out. Whatever went on between him and Marcus had drained his power. Since he'd already weakened himself when he made that fire barrier, he had to be near death. I had to do something. Now. The woodland faeries told me that they weren't able to help him because he needed to return to the eternal flame. That was the fastest way to revive a fire elemental after he'd used all his core power.

But I couldn't do it alone.

Several hounds stood outside of the barricade. Selene cried on the shoulder of one of them. They each looked on as their pack leader grieved. I ran over to them. "My knights will protect Marcus." I pointed to Rowan. "Your king needs your help."

A younger, blond-haired hound was the first to speak as we made our way over to Rowan. "Do you know how he was injured?"

"He used up all his core power," I replied, although I wasn't sure if he had other wounds. There wasn't time to check. "He may die if we don't return him to the eternal flame."

Another hound stepped forward. He picked Rowan up off the ground, cradling him in his arms. "We can take him."

"I'm going with you," I insisted.

Selene shook her head. "The flames will burn you."

"No, they won't." I opened my palm and ignited a ball of fire. They glanced at each other as they shrugged their shoulders. I peered at Rowan, lifeless in his arms. "We can't waste any more time. Show me the way to the eternal flame."

CHAPTER EIGHTEEN

MARCUS

I stood over the remnants of my wife.

A few small flecks of ash were all that remained of her. The rest had floated into the air and joined the winds. For a short moment in time, I had everything I ever wanted. I was happy. I had hope for the future. And as quickly as it came, it was ripped away from me. Leaving me torn into shreds. I had nothing. A swelling emptiness grew inside of me, creating a hole where my heart used to live. I rubbed my hands over my face as I tried to make sense of all that had happened.

When I finally stood, I realized I had knights from the air court all around me. They were each in a fighting stance as if they were prepared to defend me. I scanned the rest of the area. The ballroom was empty. The once-immaculate reception room destroyed. Blood had pooled on the floor, stained the silk linens, and even sprayed on the walls. Tables had been overturned and broken. The ceiling had burn marks and ruined light fixtures. Shards of glass were in several small piles as if someone had begun the cleanup.

I had one last mission in this world—one purpose. I'd

search until I found the elemental responsible for all of this death and destruction. The one who had started a war that cost the lives of thousands of elementals. The one that had stolen the only pure happiness I'd ever known. Rage rose within me. I'd be the one that killed him. I'd watch as the life left his eyes, and I hoped he'd experience the kind of pain I'd carry with me for the rest of my days. But I couldn't do it alone.

"Where are the hounds?" I asked one of my guards. "Where is King Rowan?"

They turned to face me in unison, lowering their weapons to their sides. "They took him to the eternal flame. He's been badly injured."

My chest burned. I couldn't take the loss of another person I loved. "Was he attacked?"

They glanced at one another as if they were searching for the answer. One of the guards stepped forward. "He passed out during the fighting."

I tried to think back to what happened after I found Ariel. A red haze covered the memories. I was still in my hound form when I tried to go after Valac. But Rowan was in my head. He used his power to stop me physically. After all these years, he discovered he inherited his mother's ability to control the hounds. It was her blood that created us. Since he was the last of her line, it made sense that he had her power. That must've been what caused him to lose consciousness.

He'd exhausted his power to save me.

I pushed my way through the knights and headed outside. The portal to the fire court was down the hill. When I stepped out the door, I gasped. The grounds were an extension of the damage I'd seen inside. I surveyed the area. It was an epic-level natural disaster. In every direction, there was more blood and destruction. Pools of water had formed several muddy pits. Trees and patches of grass were burned and torn out of the ground. Abandoned weapons and tattered fragments of clothing scattered the ground.

I had to get out of here.

Running as fast as I could, I reached the pathway in a matter of minutes. The ring of fire grew as I approached. I strode inside and kept my thoughts focused on Rowan.

THE TUNNELS BENEATH THE FIRE COURT CASTLE HAD GOTTEN easier to navigate. It hadn't been that long since I'd followed Rowan to the eternal flame. Some of my kin had traveled with us to the core of the planet to watch as he proved he was the rightful king of our court. He had no idea that the elders would return his wings. I wished I could've been there with him as it happened. A ton of guilt washed away when he flew out of the caves. Although forced, I'd never forgiven myself for leaving him disfigured. Years later, his screams still echoed in my head from that dark day.

The crackling of the burning fire was the only sound I heard. I strode down hallways with lava-covered walls so hot it steamed the air I breathed. It was like I was walking through a mile-long sauna. The temperature increased with every step. No other elemental from the other courts could withstand the heat. Even the hounds had difficulty breathing down here. As I approached the planet's core, my power rejuvenated. It had been days without much sleep, and I was desperately in need of an energy boost. The sensation was so strong I had to fight the urge to shift into my hound form.

As I approached the end of the tunnel, I saw my destination. The arena-sized cavern was a vast space held up by large rock pillars. There was no light beyond the fires burning within the molten rock. A steamy haze covered the entire cave. Members of my pack stood on the outside of a small opening. Many of them were leaning against the wall, struggling for breath. Hounds had a hard time breathing in the blistering heat-filled air, which made me wonder who had taken Rowan inside the flame.

When they saw me coming, the hounds bent their heads down as a show of respect. I did the same in return. They wouldn't mention Ariel or offer any formal condolences. Hounds rarely displayed their emotions. They were renowned for their strength and compulsion for violence, which was what I needed more than sympathy. As I headed for the small entrance, a twisting fireball spat out. I ducked a second before it nearly smacked me in the face. I poked my head inside. The flooring was nothing but pools of magma with a few flat rocks to walk along.

I couldn't make out the faces of the elementals inside. I was able to see that someone stood over a body lying on a flat surface. "Who is with Rowan?"

Ethan, the smallest and youngest of my pack, was the first to answer. "Kalin carried him inside."

I wasn't surprised. The akasha was the strongest of all the elementals. She was the only one outside of our court who could enter the flames. And she loved Rowan. I doubted there was much she wouldn't do for him. "Why couldn't he go in on his own?"

"He's still passed out," Ethan replied, eyes wide with worry. "He hasn't moved since we brought him here."

Rowan's energy should have restored well before he went inside. If he was unconscious, he must've been even worse than I thought. Closer to death than he'd ever been before. Tension filled my shoulders. I stood in the doorway, watching as he was horizontally raised at least thirty feet off the ground. A glowing ring of fire encircled him like a force field. His body jolted as worm-like flames entered his chest.

His black wings burst out, fully expanded. Then the ring of fire disappeared and fell toward the ground.

Right before he was about to hit the rock floor, he appeared to awaken. Landing on his feet, he embraced Kalin. I let out a sigh of relief. Hand in hand, they exited the eternal flame. I moved to the side, so I wasn't blocking their way. Rowan had a smile on his face until he met eyes with me. I sensed him almost as if he was reading my thoughts. Without words, he strode toward me. We embraced each other like two soldiers reuniting after a long-fought war. There was no explanation needed; nothing left to process.

I released him. "Cutting it a little close, don't you think?"

Rowan glanced back at the spitting inferno and let out an exhausted breath. "I had no other choice."

"You could've died," I cautioned. "You have to be more careful."

He smirked. "I'll keep that in mind the next time I'm saving your life."

Kalin put her arms around both of us. "This heat is intense. If you don't mind, I'd like to get out of here."

THE MOMENT WE EXITED THE PORTAL, THE HOUNDS HEADED straight for the mess hall. I followed Kalin and Rowan to his quarters. I was hungry, but we had more pressing issues. Namely, how we were going to find Valac and end his life once and for all. Blood from the battle still covered Rowan. I waited with Kalin while he showered and changed clothes. She told me that Valac had managed to steal the shield, which complicated things even further. With all four sacred objects, he was now virtually indestructible.

Killing him wasn't going to be easy. He still had rogue elementals that followed him. We'd likely have to fight our way through. After all that we'd suffered, it sounded like a daunting task. But I wouldn't rest until he was dead. Not until he paid for what he'd stolen from me. The hole in my chest ached at the thought of Ariel. How was I supposed to go on without her? Beyond retribution, I had no reason to live. She was all that I ever wanted. The only dream I ever allowed myself.

Vengeance burned in my core.

Rowan stepped out of the bathroom in a faded black Rolling Stones t-shirt and dark jeans. Wet strands of wavy hair dripped down his face. "I feel much better."

Not wanting to waste any more time, I asked, "Are you able to sense the Ring of Dispel?"

He folded his arms. "Don't you think you need some time to—?"

"Exactly my point, Rowan." I interrupted him before he could finish his sentence. The last thing I needed was more time to grieve. I'd spend the rest of my life lamenting her loss. "Valac will be expecting us to mourn, which might be our only opportunity to ambush him."

"Did you have a plan in mind?" He sat next to Kalin on his bed.

"After everything that happened, what's left of his rogue army must be exhausted," I explained. "Without access to the eternal flame, they'll need to rest. That's when we attack."

"What about the sacred objects?" Kalin asked, her eyes shifting between Rowan and me. "According to the journals, his power is infinite."

I wasn't willing to accept defeat. Not after everything I'd lost. I'd do whatever it took to see this through, and I didn't care about the cost. Nothing mattered to me anymore. My life was void.

"There's always room for mistakes," I argued. "He can't sleep in that armor. It's got to come off at some point."

"Don't you think he'll see us coming?" Rowan questioned. "It's not easy to hide an army of hounds."

I'd come up with the answer to that as well. "We won't shift until we're about to attack."

"That makes you vulnerable," Rowan spoke in a stern tone. "I'm not willing to risk your life or the lives of your pack."

"There's a risk no matter what we do." Surely he knew I understood that better than anyone. "That's the price of war."

"What do you think?" Rowan glanced at Kalin. They were both quiet as their fingers entwined. "Do you think we should attack now or wait for them to make a move?"

"Marcus is right. I doubt they'd expect an attack so soon." She turned to me with sympathy in her eyes. "But I'm worried you're going to get yourself killed."

"I can handle myself," I added quickly.

"I'm not questioning that," she smiled. "It's your demeanor. Your anger."

I stood up. "Yes, I'm angry." The words came out louder than I intended, sparking a dark glare from Rowan.

"You want revenge for Ariel." She rose to her feet. "But if that's your only motivation, you will fail."

"What is it you want me to say? Do you want me to scream? Cry? To curse the world and everyone in it?" I pushed back the pain that tried desperately to break through the wall I'd built around my heart. My tone turned desperate. "I can't do that right now. There will be no peace for me until this is over. Do you understand what I'm saying?"

Kalin reached up, cupping her hand on my cheek. Her soft touch reminded me of Ariel, and it nearly broke me. "I need to know that you're going into this with a level head."

For the whole of my life, I'd tried to be the voice of reason. The one hound that maintained a level of control, and refused to let his emotions overrule common sense. But all of that was gone now.

Pain.

Anger.

Resentment.

Vengeance.

That was all I had left. "I'll be fine. Let's gather my pack and end this."

CHAPTER NINETEEN

ROWAN

I prepared for the final battle.

While Marcus showered and changed, I made the pack aware of our plans. Based on the reports from the hounds, only a few rogues had survived the last attack. We didn't need big numbers for the ambush. That was why we decided not to make the other courts aware of our decision. They'd want to rush in with all that we had. I didn't want to risk Valac figuring it out and escaping again. For that reason, we'd go in with only the hounds in their mortal forms. Once we were ready to strike, they'd shift.

I was heading toward the weapons storehouse when I ran into Merlin. He'd cleaned himself up since I last saw him. His face was shaven, and he wore modern clothing: a simple long-sleeved maroon shirt and dark jeans. We stood silent for a few uncomfortable seconds. I wasn't sure what to say to him after our last conversation. It certainly hadn't ended well.

"Kalin told me about your plans," he said, ending the awkward silence. "I'm coming with you."

I wasn't surprised she had. She'd wanted me to speak

with Merlin since she'd learned he was my father. But I wasn't ready to do the open-arms thing. I didn't downshift that quickly. And I wasn't really into bonding. He was my father, but what did that mean? I didn't know anything about him. And what I had learned was more than I could handle. It seemed easier to keep him at a distance, at least until we got through this.

"We don't need you," I answered smugly.

"You needed me in the air court," he argued, crossing his arms. "I was regenerated. I could've helped you."

He was probably right. I'd let my anger get in the way when I'd refused to let him attend Marcus's wedding. Had Merlin been there, he would've likely saved many lives. I sighed. "There's no point in discussing what might've happened. We need to deal with what is."

"I agree," he replied, with a smirk on his face. "I'll meet the rest of you in the throne room in five minutes."

He walked away before I had a chance to respond.

Stubborn ass.

I made my way to the weapons storage. Once inside, I snapped my fingers. Each candle in the room illuminated. Every weapon available on Avalon filled the large room to the brim. The walls were lined with swords, knives, and bows with iron-tipped arrows in every shape and size. Glass bottles filled with explosives were lined up on a wooden table in the center of the room. The hounds didn't need weapons, but I wanted to be cautious in case we were surprised.

Marcus had me worried. It wasn't like him to jump into something drastic. He wasn't himself. The cautious friend I'd known all of my life was full of anger and rage. Since I'd learned to communicate with him in his animal form, I was now able to sense his emotions. I tried to tap into him as we spoke, but all I sensed was his desire for revenge. The absence of anything else scared the life out of me. I considered canceling the whole thing. The only reason I hadn't already was because we'd miss an opportunity if we waited.

I collected a variety of weapons into a canvas bag I found hanging on the wall. I thrust the sack over my shoulder and winced. The damn thing weighed a ton. Once I reached the throne room, at least a hundred hounds filled nearly every available space. Not all of them were coming. Families said their goodbyes to their fathers and older siblings. It was one of the only times I'd witnessed any show of emotion from them. The hounds were especially secretive of their rules and customs. Being best friends with their leader got me closer than any other before me, but I'd never been one of them.

As I laid the blades across a table, Selene timidly approached. Instead of the servant's clothing I'd gotten used to seeing her in, she changed into leather pants and a black tank top. As if that weren't strange enough, she grabbed a sword out of my bag and swung it a few times. It was hard to believe this was the same girl who spent decades strolling around the castle in lavish gowns like some old-fashioned princess. "What are you planning to do with that sword?"

"I'm going with you," she replied, standing firm.

I chuckled. "Are you in the mood to die today?"

She let out a banshee scream that brought me to my knees but didn't affect any of the hounds. They watched as I held my hands to my ears, trying to block the sound as much as possible. The screeching noise felt like someone was drilling a screw into my head. When I was sure my ears were about to bleed, she abruptly stopped. "Any more questions?"

"Nope." My ears still rang. "You're going."

Grinning, she headed back over to a group of female hounds. I'd always assumed she was an untrained banshee. In the years I'd known her, she'd never expressed any interest in learning. She was the weaker twin, always following Valac's every move. But she had total control of her pitch. I massaged my temples.

That would be the last time I underestimated her.

Kalin and Marcus rushed into the room. Winds blew around her like a tornado. Her hair whipped all over the place as she scanned the area. Everyone watched them, wondering what was going on. When everyone went back to what they were doing, she shut it down. "What was that noise?"

"That was Selene," I replied, sounding as surprised as they looked.

Marcus scratched his head. "I thought she was untrained."

I pinched the bridge of my nose as I recalled the searing pain. "Oh yeah, she's trained."

Kalin let out a sigh of relief. "I'm glad she's on our side."

Banshees were rare in the elemental world. Like incubi, they had a very dangerous power. Centuries ago, many were hunted and killed off once they determined they were too wild to be controlled. Some had gotten a little more creative. They developed iron collars that dulled their abilities, which made it easier to turn them into servants. I believed that was why their birth mother gave them to Prisma. She was strong enough to protect the twins and appreciated the potential of Selene's power. Luckily for them, she grew to love them, and raised them as part of the royal family.

A familiar humming rang in my ear. I headed outside, away from all the noise in the throne room. It was the Ring of Dispel. Once more, it was trying to communicate with me. Like last time, I closed my eyes and concentrated on the sound. The buzzing grew louder as an image came into focus. The ring was in the woodland forests close to the fire court border. In the distance, I saw a glowing shimmer. It was the mist. My chest tightened. Valac was preparing to follow through on his threat. I'd bet he planned to wait there until he heard from the leaders of the courts. If we refused to pledge our allegiance to him, he'd cut the mist protecting Avalon.

I gazed up at the skies. We had a few hours left before sunrise. If we were going to ambush them, we needed to do it soon. I came back inside and waved over Marcus and Kalin. "I know where he's keeping the ring."

Marcus nodded. "I'll gather the hounds and weapons."

Kalin grabbed my hand, entwining our fingers. "Are you sure you want to do this?"

My eyebrows knit together. "Are you worried we won't succeed?"

"No, I'm worried about Marcus." She glanced over at him as he directed his pack. "I'm afraid he might do something reckless."

I held her hand to my lips and kissed her knuckles. "I'll protect Marcus."

She unsheathed my sword with her other hand and ignited the blade with blue fire. "And I'll protect you."

I used to think that a woman in stilettos was the hottest thing on the planet. I was wrong. My badass girlfriend swinging a sword was the sexiest thing I'd ever seen. She leaned in and kissed me as if she were reading my thoughts. I hoped she didn't have that power because my thoughts about her weren't usually the gentlemanly type.

After the weapons were passed out and the goodbyes were said, we strode toward the pathway. I considered traveling by foot, but the fire territory was mostly a flat surface with very little to conceal us. It was better to use a portal to get into the woodland territory. Once we were in the forest, lots of trees and a variety of greenery would keep us covered. As we made our way, Kalin stayed by my side near the back of our group. Selene remained close to Marcus at the front of the line. They didn't speak much. I was surprised by their friendship, especially when she was prepared to sacrifice herself to protect him.

Selene wasn't at all the way I'd pictured her.

She'd been weak and spoiled, but being around the hounds had helped her to see our world differently. Now she understood the injustice of their forced servitude. I was proud of her for that. Over the last few days, she'd gone against her brother, defended Marcus, and comforted Ariel in her final moments. Not to mention how she entertained and served the hounds when she first returned to the castle. It made me hopeful that we could resolve our differences and learn how to be siblings. As I continued to watch them, Merlin caught up to us. Kalin smiled at me, then sped up to walk beside Selene.

Sneaky little minx.

Merlin kept his eyes forward as we strode together. "Not something I'd ever expected to see."

I chuckled. "Agreed."

"I think it's good for them both," he said, keeping pace with me. "Marcus needs a friend right now."

"Marcus has friends," I corrected him with aggravation in my tone. "He always has."

Ignoring my remarks, he replied, "I'm sorry about Ariel. I know she was loved by many."

"How would you know?" I questioned, then thought about it for a second. I remembered what he told me about his power. "Oh, let me guess. You were spying on me again."

He moved in front of me and pivoted. "I never used my power to spy on you. You're my son, Rowan. I wanted to know you."

Now I felt like an asshole. I never intended to give Merlin such a hard time. It had been weird for me. The idea that I'd had a father all along, and he'd been watching me throughout my whole life. But it was more than that. He'd given me information about my mother that I'd never heard from anyone else. It was hard to believe she'd done all those horrible things to protect me. That all along, she loved me. That she had grown to be wicked because she was lonely and filled with grief over imprisoning my father.

"There are things that need to be said, and I know I'm difficult." I let out a long sigh. "Let's get through this, and then I'll make time." I put my hand on his shoulder. "In the meantime, I'll try not to be such a shithead."

He chuckled. "Sounds good to me, Son."

Son.

It meant a lot more to me than I'd ever let anyone know. "Come on, let's go join the rest of the group."

I FOLLOWED THE RING'S SIGNAL TO A SMALL GROUP OF TENTS in the middle of a thick brush. The ring would protect them from Orion's power. He had no idea Valac and his rogues were camped out in the corner of his territory. Luckily, Valac hadn't figured out that I had a connection to the ring. If he knew that, he'd never be out in the open. I scanned the surrounding area as much as I could. The only light was the moon, which barely shone through the trees. The hounds were busy shifting into their animal form. They were as quiet as they could be, but I heard their bones cracking during the change.

If Valac wasn't asleep, he'd heard them too.

Once their shift was complete, they waited for my signal. I held my hand up in the air, then thrust it back down. We charged on the rogues as a group. The hounds growled as they approached, shaking the ground beneath our feet. Some of us struggled to keep our balance. I was the first to reach their camp. I raised my sword and slid the blade through the slim canvas tent, and I peered inside. It was empty. There was a bustling outside of the abandoned campground. I heard the pounding of feet. Then, they appeared all around us. We were trapped.

They had tricked us.

Several hundred rogues surrounded us. That meant Valac hadn't sent his entire army to the air court. He'd kept these soldiers behind. As they ran toward us, the hounds went on the attack. Kalin used her wind magic to push many of them back. But even she couldn't hold them all. Soon, we were in the midst of another battle. The hounds tore into them, ripping them apart piece by piece. They were smart, though. They attacked each hound in groups, trying to overpower them. So far, it wasn't working.

"Can you stop them?" I yelled to Selene.

"There are too many." Her eyes were wide with fear. "If I scream, it will knock everyone out at once."

Taking us all out wasn't an option. "Stand back, then. Use it only if you have to. Focus your scream on anyone who attacks you."

"Okay." She nodded her head, then ran to hide behind a group of twisted trees.

I swung my sword, inviting them to challenge me. I was fighting two and three rogues at a time. They relied mostly on their fire magic. They wouldn't last long. Each time they used their flames, their inner core weakened. Once I saw my opportunity, I sliced and diced my way through each one. As the fight raged on, I searched for Valac. Once again, he was hiding in the darkness. He hadn't left. I felt the presence of the ring. "Come on, Valac," I teased. "Show yourself."

No answer.

I searched for Kalin. One of the rogues shot a line of fire toward her. She used water magic to put out the flame, then slid her blade through his chest. He fell to the ground at her feet. When she turned to face me, she had blood sprayed on the side of her face. I wiped it off with my palm. "You're so hot right now."

She rolled her eyes. "You're ridiculous."

"You love it."

Now that I knew she was safe, I fought my way over to Marcus. I caught a glimpse of him as he leaped on top of a group of rogues, tearing into their necks with his teeth. Merlin stood behind him, protecting his back while Marcus finished them off. I glanced at the perimeter. The rogues kept coming. This situation was playing out as it had at the wedding. I had to put an end to this. I had to find Valac. I tried to drown out all the noise and focus on the ring. After a moment, I heard the buzz coming from the woods thirty yards away. I cut my way through at least ten more rogues before I made it into the darkest part of the forest.

I ignited an orb of fire in my palm.

Something snapped behind me. I spun around and ducked a second before Valac could get a piece of me. He wore the armor and held Excalibur. I gripped my sword tighter and went after him. "Trying to stab me in the back? That's low even for you."

Our weapons screeched as they scraped together. "It doesn't matter how you die as long as you're dead."

He pushed away from me, putting distance between us. We circled each other. "There's no one around to help you," I taunted. "I guess that means you'll have to do some dirty work for a change."

"I don't need help killing you." He held up Excalibur, reminding me of his advantage.

I waved him on, goading him. "Then what are you waiting for?"

Growling, he lunged at me. I twisted out of the way, and he fell to the ground. I thrust my sword down over the top of him, but he rolled away at the last possible second. "Those are some fancy moves you got there," I mocked. "I think I saw that on a cartoon once."

He swatted at me from the ground, and I jumped to avoid his blade. "After you're dead, I'm going to skin those hounds and use their hides to decorate my chambers."

I rushed him. "You'll have to kill me first."

Now on his feet, he blocked my charge. "That's my plan."

Our swords clashed as we took turns attacking each other. It was more of a joust than a fight to the death. Neither of us had done any damage. He managed to keep up with me as the minutes rolled past. Excalibur had been responsible for his newly discovered swordsmanship. He'd never been physically strong. He'd never kept up with me before, not even when I was little more than a child. I tested a few maneuvers on him, trying to get the weapon out of his hand. He used the shield to block my efforts. "You ought to see how well you do without all of the sacred objects. You should show the rogues what a poor choice they made."

"Why would I do that when I'm winning?" he replied, coming at me hard and thrashing his sword against mine.

Valac tried to slide his blade toward the grip of my sword, hoping he might scratch me. I pushed him back. He didn't need to beat me. All he had to do was cut my skin. But his pride kept him fighting, which I hoped to use against him. "Going for the easy kill? Am I surprised? Not really."

The hounds close to me were doing much better. As a group, they took on forty or fifty rogues at a time. I hadn't seen any loses on our side, but I did notice the rogues scattered on the ground in chewed-up pieces. There was so much blood everywhere that it almost didn't seem real, like something out of an old horror movie before they had all the cool special effects.

As the fighting went on, he noticed I was breathing heavily. I wasn't out of breath. I was close, though. I wasn't sure how much more of his non-stop assault I'd be able to handle. "I'm wearing you down, Rowan."

A hound came out of nowhere. It was Marcus. He bit into Valac's wrist, sinking his teeth in deep. The Green Armor protected Valac, but he couldn't get free. "Get off of me, beast," he screamed.

Marcus wouldn't let up. He swung his head, trying to loosen his grip on the sword. Valac tried striking him in the face with the shield. I joined the fight, holding onto the shield and preventing him from hitting Marcus. Merlin appeared out of the corner of my eye. He put his enflamed hands over Valac's fists, trying to burn the sword out of his hands. "You found Merlin?" he snarled. "It doesn't matter. Magic protects me."

Valac reached for a small knife hidden within the sleeve of his armor. He tried to cut me with it, but he couldn't move his arm without releasing the shield. "Let go of the shield and take your shot," I said, provoking him.

A shrieking scream filled the air. It was the loudest banshee call I'd ever heard. Selene appeared out of the dark forest, aiming all her power at us. There was no stopping her. I fell to my knees, pressing my hands over my ears. Her song drilled into me, and I froze from the pain. Marcus glanced at me. Her scream blocked my ability to hear his thoughts, but somehow I knew he was going to give the sword one final tug. When he dug his teeth into the Green Armor, Valac screamed out in agony. Blood spewed. I saw that Marcus had bent the metal into his arm. With his jaws locked, he shook Valac's wrist with all his remaining strength. Excalibur went flying in the air.

Selene stopped and gasped with her hands over her mouth.

I struggled to get to my feet. When I finally managed, I

pushed my way through the remaining rogues. Everyone stared up into the sky. I raised my eyes. High above us, the mist held the buried sword. A crack about a foot long had sprung out of both sides with little shards of flickering light leaking down to the ground. Kalin burst out of the crowd and into my arms. I held her tight as her tears ran down the back of my neck.

It was over.

CHAPTER TWENTY

KALIN

We'd won the battle but lost the war.

Excalibur remained embedded within the mist, which had already started to crack. Sparkling bits of magic leaked from the growing hole. At some point, Valac had retreated along with the few rogues that survived. No one went after them. Why bother? There was nothing more to fight over. Within hours the mist would be no more, exposing Avalon to the rest of the mortal world. All the older elementals would soon begin to rapidly age as time caught up with them. Thousands would be dead within hours, including Orion, Marlena, and Britta.

But I wouldn't let that happen. I'd save everyone. It was as the spirit of the akasha had told me. My blood was the key. I had accepted the truth after I'd left the temple. I was ready for the sacrifice. Saying goodbye to all of my friends would be the toughest part. Saying goodbye to my mother would be excruciating. Without any other family, I was all she had left in this world. Where would she choose to live once I was gone? Would she ever recover after losing my father, and, soon, her only child?

And what about Rowan?

How was I supposed to say goodbye to him? I dug my fingers into his shirt. I wanted to soak in every last moment with him. Memorize the feel of his arms around me. The smell of his skin. The sound of his voice. Tears ran down my cheeks in streams. How would I make him understand what I had to do? He'd fought so hard to find another solution. I went all over our world in an attempt to save my life. Would he accept my sacrifice? Would he stand in my way? Would he move on?

I had so much to do in only a few short hours. My heart sank as I let go of Rowan. "I have to find my mother. She doesn't know about any of this." He appeared surprised, so I elaborated. "I didn't want to tell her. I was holding out hope that we'd find another way."

With desperation in his eyes, he replied, "Maybe we still can."

I caressed his cheek as I swallowed the lump in my throat. No matter how grim the circumstances, he never gave up on me. He'd always been my hero. "We both know it's time to tell her."

He wrapped his arms around me, burying his face in my shoulder. "I don't know how to let you go."

"This is what I have to do." I leaned my head against him, closing my eyes. "I'm sorry. I hope you'll one day understand."

"There's something I can do," Merlin said, surprising us both. I hadn't realized he was standing there. I thought we were alone.

"You told me you couldn't stop it," Rowan replied, releasing me from his hold.

"I can't heal the mist." Merlin met eyes with me. His tone was soft and full of grief. "But I can give you time to say your goodbyes."

"How?" I asked.

"The mist was created using my magic and the blood of the akasha. The mist can absorb my power and heal itself for some time." Merlin glared up at the crack, growing larger as each minute passed. "You'll have twelve hours at the most."

As the sun rose in the sky, a rainbow-colored shimmer illuminated the mist. It was beautiful and powerful and otherworldly, all at the same time. Merlin had spent the last eighteen years in a frozen cage, and days afterward would give his life so that we might have a few hours to say good-bye. It was a massive sacrifice for such a small amount of time. But it meant the world to me. Now I would be able to say goodbye to the people I loved properly. I took his hands in mine. "Thank you."

"Wait." Rowan held up his hand as he tried to come to grips with what was happening. "What do you mean by absorbing your power? Are you saying—?"

Merlin smiled weakly at Rowan. "Yes, I will also have to sacrifice myself."

His skin paled. "I'm not going to stand here and watch you both die." He shook his head, refusing to accept what he'd heard.

Leaves rustled, and Marcus appeared out of the thick brush in his mortal form. Blood had stained his face and clothes. As soon as he saw the sword, he smashed his fist into the nearest tree trunk. "No," he growled.

I made my way over, putting my hand on his shoulder. "It will all be okay soon."

His eyes were wild as he yelled, "Things will never be okay ever again."

I put my hand over my chest, sensing his agony. "That's not what I meant."

Marcus pushed me away, putting distance between us. "I'm sorry, Kalin." Tears ran down his cheeks. "I was trying to get him to drop the sword. I hadn't expected it to thrust out of his hand. I—"

"What are you talking about?" Rowan asked as a tear ran down his cheek.

"This is all my fault," Marcus replied in barely a whisper.

"You can't blame yourself," Rowan said, eyes rounded. "I won't let you carry that burden."

"Hours ago, I held Ariel in my arms as she died. I watched *my wife* take her last breath." He barely managed to get the words out as he struggled to hold himself together. "She gave her life to save Kalin. And now, Kalin's going to die because of me." He motioned toward the battlefield filled with decomposing bodies. "All the fighting we've done. All of the death and destruction. It was all for nothing," he shouted. "Even if we won, we lost everything that mattered."

Rowan attempted to reach out to him, but he held his hand up. Marcus strode over and put his arms around me. "I'm sorry I failed you."

"No, you didn't," I whispered in his ear. He'd fought hard. I didn't hold him responsible for what happened. It was a fluke at best. There was no reason for him to apologize.

Marcus wiped his tears away with the back of his hand. Without saying another word, he trudged back into the thick forest. He was heading in the direction of the fire court. Selene was about to go after him when Rowan asked, "Where are you going?"

"He shouldn't be alone right now." Selene lowered her gaze to the ground. "Even if he doesn't know it, he needs a friend."

"You barely know him," Rowan argued.

Her arms hung loosely at her sides as she let out an exhausted breath. "You're right. I haven't known him for very long, but I care about him. He means something to me. And even though I know I don't deserve him, Marcus is my friend."

"Go," Rowan said, waving his hand in dismissal. There was no fight left in him.

The corner of her lip rose, then she ran after Marcus. Selene and Rowan had a lot that needed to be said. After the pain of my sacrifice passed, I hope they find a way to be friends. In the short time I'd known her, she'd turned out to be one of the bravest elementals I'd ever known. And she showed me that people could change. Marcus was a big part of that. I prayed they'd all lean on each other for support once I was gone.

Merlin approached Rowan. "This is where I must say goodbye."

"Does it have to be right now?" he asked in a panicked tone. "We never even had a chance to talk."

He glared up at the expanding hole. "Every minute I wait will leave you one less with Kalin." Merlin clasped his hand around his biceps. "I want to give you this gift. I only wish I could do more."

Rowan put his arms around him. "I don't know what to say."

Merlin pulled back. "I want you to know there hasn't been a second in your life that you were alone. I've always been by your side. Through all the challenges and despair, you managed to defy the odds. I am in awe of the leader that you've become. I am a proud father." He made his way over to the mist, pressing his hands into the hazy glow. Looking over his shoulder, he said, "I love you, Son."

"I love you too, Dad," Rowan replied, sniffling.

Merlin smiled as he slowly faded away. It only took a few moments before he was fully absorbed. There was a rumble, and Excalibur slid out of the opening and landed at Rowan's feet. I took a glimpse at the tear. Magic no longer drizzled down from the hole. He sealed the crack, but the scarred remnants were still visible. What he'd done wouldn't solve the problem, but he had given us some time.

I glanced at Rowan as he picked up the sword. Dumbfounded was the only word that would explain the look on his face. "Is he gone?"

I bit my lip and nodded. "I'm sorry."

"I wouldn't speak to him. I didn't believe him. I pushed him away," he rambled. "And now he's gone."

I wrapped my arms around his neck, and we crumpled to the ground together. As I held onto him, I was prepared to stay as long as he needed me to be there. The rest of the world faded away. And neither of us said another word.

THERE WAS NO EASY OR RIGHT WAY TO SAY GOODBYE TO MY mother. As I made my way through the portal, I thought about different ways I could tell her I was about to die. Nothing I'd come up with seemed like it would lessen the blow. When I reached the air court castle, I was shocked to discover the completely restored landscape. The trees had healed along with the burned grass. Flowering hills replaced the muddied piles of abandoned weaponry, leaving no evidence of a battle anywhere. I stepped inside and discovered the fully renovated ballroom: no more broken tables or bloodied floors. Even the wedding decorations were gone.

Whoever had done this must've worked tirelessly throughout the night.

As I was about to leave, my mother surprised me. She stepped out of the kitchen, wiping her hands on a clean rag. She hadn't realized I'd come home. A lump swelled in my throat. How was I ever going to get through this? "What are you doing down here?"

She startled, and then she ran over and threw her arms around me. "I was so worried about you. When the attack started, the guards insisted I go to my room. They wouldn't let me out." She took my face in her hands as she checked for injuries. "When it was over, you were gone."

"I'm sorry I didn't get a message to you." Everything happened so fast. I hadn't even thought about it, which made me feel awful. "Rowan was hurt, and he had to be taken to the fire court to heal."

"Is he all right?" she asked, her tone full of concern.

Rowan was falling apart. The father he never knew gave his life for us. And now he had to prepare for my death. But I couldn't speak of that yet. Instead, I answered only about his physical health. "Yes, he's fine now."

She cringed. "I heard what happened to Ariel. How is Marcus?"

"Pretty much how you'd expect." There was only one word that came to my mind. "Broken."

"Her parents are devastated. Ariel had sent them away after the fighting started." She glanced at the spot where Ariel had died. "They got back here around the same time I did."

I wasn't sure how I was going to say it, but now was the time. "Mom, there's something I have to tell you."

Her forehead creased. "What is it, sweetheart?"

I tried to simplify what happened as much as possible. There was no need to fill in all of the gory details. I told Mom what I thought she most needed to know. "After we took Rowan to the eternal flame, we decided to go after Valac. We thought he wouldn't be expecting an attack so soon after Ariel's death. We were wrong. There was a big fight, and a lot of elementals died."

She held her hand up to her lips. "Oh, no."

I reached for a chair at a nearby table. "Would you sit down for a minute?"

"No," she replied firmly. "Whatever it is, tell me now."

My chest tightened. "A sacred sword pierced the mist that protects Avalon. Once it's gone, thousands of elementals will die. But there's a way I can save them."

"How?" she asked.

I took in a deep breath and then slowly let it out as I prepared to say the words that would break her heart. "The blood of the akasha can seal the tear. All of my blood."

Tears welled in her eyes. "Are you telling me you have to die to save the others?"

Unable to say any more, I nodded.

She pulled me into a tight embrace as the tears trickled down her cheeks. "I can't let you do that."

"You don't have a choice," I replied, battling the tears that threatened to release. I had to hold it together for my mother. "I wondered why I received these powers. Why I became the akasha, but now I know. This sacrifice was my purpose."

She released me, wiping her nose with the kitchen rag. "We can leave. We'll search for a hideaway somewhere in the mortal world. Someplace where they'd never find you."

"I can't run away." I swallowed the lump in my throat. "The world will end if the balance isn't brought back to the elements. I have to do this."

"I don't care about the elements or anyone else for that matter." She fell to her knees, sobbing into her hands. "All I care about is you."

I'd never seen her lose it like this. My heart shattered into pieces as I watched her, knowing I was the cause. If I had any other choice, I would've taken it. There was none. My only comfort was knowing I was doing the right thing. Giving my life to save thousands was an easy choice to make. It might take her months, or maybe even years, but I had faith she'd realize that one day.

I got down on my knees and pulled her into a hug. "I swear if there were another way I'd take it. But there isn't. I've searched the akasha journals, and Rowan found the creator of the mist. He confirmed this was the only way."

Mom pulled away, and her eyes narrowed. "Wait, how long have you known about this?"

"I discovered this was a possibility shortly after I gained my akasha powers."

Her eyebrows raised. "And you decided not to tell me? Why?"

"You were grieving. I thought this would've been too much for you to handle." I lowered my gaze. "I'm sorry."

"You shouldn't have done that, Kalin," she argued. "I could've helped you. Maybe we could've found another way together."

"There is no other way, Mom. We've exhausted every option," I assured her, as I tried to help her off the floor. "I have to do this."

"I don't accept that," She replied as she rose to her feet with determination in her tone. "I never will. We have to keep trying. There has to be some other way. Maybe we can ask Orion or Britta."

I shook my head. "Orion and Britta are both aware of the circumstances. There's nothing either of them can do."

"I won't lose my little girl," she sniffled. "There has to be something I can do."

This news was too much for her to bear. No matter what I said, she wasn't prepared to accept that this was going to happen. I found myself overcome with worry for her. What would happen to her once I was gone? How could I guarantee her safety? I had an idea. A way to protect her after I was gone. "You can make me a promise."

"What's that?"

With a firm tone, I replied, "I want you to rule the air court in my place."

"You can't be serious." Her eyes rounded. "I'm not an elemental."

"Neither am I." I'd come to Avalon as a halfling. And then, I'd become the akasha. I held her hand. "You're the bravest, strongest mortal I know. This court will flourish under your rule."

"The court of air won't need a new ruler because you're not going anywhere." She placed her hands on her hips. "I won't stand by and watch you sacrifice yourself."

I let out an exaggerated sigh.

There was no point in going back and forth with her. "I have to go. I'm sorry."

"What?" She shrieked. "You can't go now."

"I have to meet with the council so that I can name you as my successor." Her ascension would be my final decree as the queen of this court. The council had no choice in the matter. Every one of them would die within hours if I didn't sacrifice myself.

"So that's it? I'm supposed to say goodbye?" She waved her hands wildly. "Is that what's happening here?"

Tears ran down my cheeks. "I don't know what else I can say."

Mom didn't say another word as she turned and walked away. I didn't chase after her. These final moments didn't go the way I planned. I'd expected too much from her. I should've known she wasn't capable of saying goodbye. What mother could? She needed more time to accept what was happening.

But time was the one thing I didn't have.

CHAPTER TWENTY-ONE

MARCUS

I wanted to end the agony.

We'd gone into this war with the best of intentions. We wanted to bring balance back to the elements and save lives. But all we'd managed to do was bring pain and death to the ones we loved the most. I didn't want to live in a world without Ariel. She was everything to me. And now, she was gone. Without her, I'd completely lost my will to live. She'd made the ultimate sacrifice, giving her life to save Kalin.

But it was all for nothing.

I was so desperate to kill Valac that I made a critical mistake. When I dug my teeth into his wrist and shook him with all my strength, Excalibur flew into the air. The sword cut the mist, and now Kalin's life would end. She would die because of my error, my rash decision. Rowan saw the whole thing. Once he got past the initial shock, he would realize that this was all my fault. I wouldn't blame him if he wanted to end my life.

Death was what I deserved.

Hearing footsteps behind me, I swirled around. It was

Selene. She must've tracked me back here. No matter. "I don't need you to follow me around. I'm fine." No, I wasn't fine. I was out of my mind. Grief and regret flowed through me in waves, making it hard to breathe. "Don't worry about me."

She stayed on my tail as I moved through the winding obsidian walkways, totally ignoring what I'd said. I let out an aggravated growl, trying to scare her off. She was unfazed, didn't even flinch. I tried to increase my pace. Each time, she caught up. When I reached my bedroom, I closed the door behind me. The message was loud and clear.

I glanced down at my clothing and sighed. Blood was everywhere. Before I shifted, I had time to remove my clothes. But I'd put them back on after the battle, and now the shirt and pants were ruined. I slipped them off, throwing both pieces in a nearby wastebasket. I headed into the bathroom and bent over the sink. Using a liquid cleanser, I scrubbed soap on my hands and face.

"I'm not leaving you alone," she yelled from the hallway. "I'll stay out here all day and night if I have to."

I dried my face with a hand towel. This girl was stubborn. It was a family trait. "You're as annoying as Rowan," I shouted.

I heard her laugh. "Then you know I'm not going anywhere."

I rolled my eyes.

"Let me in already," she pleaded. "I feel ridiculous talking to you like this."

There was no getting rid of her. I changed into a plain white shirt and jeans, then strode to the door and opened it. "What do you want?"

Her eyes rounded. "I came to support my friend."

I crossed my arms. "What if your friend wants to be alone?"

"I want to talk about what you said back there," she replied, ignoring my question.

I tried to shut the door, but she held it open. "There's nothing left to say."

"Yes, there is." She pushed her way inside my room. "Valac is responsible for the mist getting cut. Not you."

That wasn't true. It was my fault. I wasn't paying attention or even considering that the sword might fly out of Valac's hand. I was too caught up in my pain. It was like I could think of nothing else but revenge. I turned away from her. "You didn't see what happened."

"It doesn't matter." She tried to comfort me, putting her palm on my shoulder blade. "You wouldn't have been there in the first place had it not been for my brother. He's to blame for everything."

As I replayed the events that led up to our failed ambush, I placed my hands over my face. "We were there because of me. I convinced Rowan to go after Valac. I was so angry and miserable that I wasn't thinking clearly."

"You did what you thought was right," she tried to assure me in a soft tone. "No one blames you for what happened."

The image of Rowan holding Kalin as she cried flashed in my mind. "Maybe not now, but someday he will. He'll be immersed in the pain of Kalin's loss and realize it was his best friend who took away the love of his life."

"You're wrong." She shifted around and lowered my hands. "Rowan knows who you are. He'd never believe that."

I shook my head. "You don't know him the way I do."

She cupped my shoulders and waited until I met her eyes before she spoke. "I know that he needs you right now. He's about to lose someone he loves, and the one person who can understand that pain won't be there."

I lowered my gaze to the floor. "I can't face Rowan right now."

"He *needs* you, Marcus," she repeated in a persistent tone with her hands on her hips. "Now, more than ever. So you have to decide if you're going to stay here and feel sorry for yourself or be there for your best friend."

I chuckled. "You're a lot tougher than you let on."

She grinned as she punched me in the arm. "Only when I need to smack some sense into my friends."

Selene was right. After Prisma forced me to tear off Rowan's wings, I couldn't deal with what had happened. I'd left him a note and asked that he not try to find me. During my absence, he'd gotten hurt and nearly died. When I returned, I had sworn to him that I'd never leave his side again. I won't go back on my promise. I refused to abandon him again. Not when his circumstances were disastrous.

I let out an exaggerated sigh.

"I'll go back, but I want to wait a while." I thought back to Ariel's final moments. How Kalin had ordered her knights to surround us, so we weren't disturbed. I owed her the same in return. "They need some time alone. Trust me. It's for the best."

Her eyebrows furrowed. "What should we do in the meantime?"

My stomach growled so loud, she laughed. "I think I've got an idea."

The light illuminated the mess hall when we entered it. It was surprisingly empty. On any other day, hounds were here in droves. But I had already put the pack on high alert. Most of them were on guard, and the rest had taken their families to safety. Hounds were strong at any age, but anyone unable to fight had to leave. This situation was only temporary. Once Valac was found and killed, I'd have them all return. It was strange being here when there was no noise.

"Looks like we're on our own." I scratched my stubble. "I don't suppose you know how to cook."

"Come on." She grabbed my hand and led me toward the kitchen.

I observed the way she searched through cabinets. It was only the second time she'd been here, but she moved around like she knew where everything was. I sat on a stool in front of the large chopping block while she sliced several pieces of fruit. When she finished, she set the plate in front of me with utensils and a napkin. I gobbled everything up within minutes. While I ate, she put together a variety of bread and cheese. The assortment of smells made my stomach rumble. I couldn't remember the last time I'd eaten. Everything happened so fast after the wedding.

It was a daze.

When she brought the final plate over, she sat on the stool next to me. I watched while she placed a napkin in her lap, then cut her bread into bite-sized pieces. She held her utensils delicately, and her movements seemed rehearsed. She had some formal etiquette lessons. It was the opposite of the hounds. Table manners weren't part of our training. We were loud and ate mostly with our hands, and it wasn't uncommon to see several of us with food all over our faces.

"Are you feeling any better? I mean, since we talked?" she asked, right before she took her first bite.

"I don't know." I shrugged, swallowing a mouth full of bread. I didn't know what to say. The love of my life was gone, and every dream I had for my life went with her. Now I was alone in this world. I had no direction. "It still hurts."

Selene pushed the food around her plate. "You know you can talk to me about her, right?"

I had no words. The only thing I felt was the overwhelming emptiness of Ariel's loss. "I'm good for now."

"Well, I'm here." She glanced over at me, then back to her plate. "If there's ever anything you want to say."

I glanced down at her plate. "Why aren't you eating?"

"I am." She put another small bite of bread in her mouth.

"You barely touched anything on your plate," I noted. "You've got to be hungry."

"We were always taught to take our time," she replied, smearing soft cheese on a chunk of crust.

All her movements were careful like she feared she'd make a mistake. Like someone was watching and judging her every move. For once in her life, I wanted her to relax. "Well, you're one of us now, so cancel all that proper shit."

"Okay," she laughed. "How am I supposed to eat?"

"Like this." I tore a big hunk of bread off the loaf and stuffed it in my mouth. "You try."

Her eyebrows raised. "I can't do that."

I took a cue from her. Using her knife, I delicately cut the rest of the loaf into even slices. Each portion was half the size of what I'd stuffed in my mouth. When I was finished playfully mocking her, I smeared cheese on a section and held it out in front of her. "Open wide."

With a broad smile on her face, she shook her head. "No way."

I rolled my eyes. "Why? You don't trust me?"

She pointed her finger at me. "I'm only taking a bite."

"Okay," I assured her.

As soon as she opened her mouth, I stuffed the whole piece inside. Her eyes widened with surprise, and I couldn't help laughing.

She playfully smacked my arm as she tried to chew.

Ethan ran into the kitchen with a frantic look on his face. As soon as I saw him, I stood. "What's wrong?"

"We're under attack," he replied, with wild eyes. "Rogues have entered the castle. I'm not sure how many, but I've gotten reports from three different locations."

Valac. He sustained injuries during our fight. With every other court searching for him, he had nowhere else to go. No other elemental would offer him any healing herbs or ointments. He had to return to the eternal flame. And there was only one way to get there. "Send reinforcements to every location. I'm heading down to the portal."

Ethan's eyebrows knit together. "You're not going to join the counterattack?"

"This is a diversion." Valac didn't care about the rogues. He'd sent them into battle, knowing most wouldn't survive. There was no question in my mind. He'd sacrifice every last one of them to heal himself. "He's heading for the eternal flame."

"Only the king of the fire court can enter the flame," Ethan argued, with a look of confusion on his face.

Rowan had once challenged Valac to enter, but he refused. If he entered the flames, they'd likely destroy him for what he'd done, but he could heal if he managed to get close enough to the caverns outside of the entrance. The power should be enough to repair him or at least get him to the point where he started to self-heal. "He doesn't have to go inside. He needs to get close."

"I'll go with you," Ethan replied as fire flashed in his eyes.

"We'll all go," Selene added.

The moment I'd waited for had finally come to fruition. Killing Valac wouldn't bring Ariel back or heal the aching hole her loss had left in my heart, but it would end his war against the courts. That was enough for me. "No, he's mine."

Ethan and Selene continued to offer their assistance while I shifted into my hound form. I didn't hear a word either said. I was too focused on my mission. I had to get to him fast. The closer he got to the flames, the harder it would be for me to breathe. That gave him an advantage. He would also get stronger as he healed.

Along with the shield and armor, that wasn't going to be easy. I had to be smart about every move I made. I couldn't risk Ethan's lack of experience or Selene's love for her brother.

I rushed through hallways and downstairs until I reached the pathway. The hound I'd stationed down here was dead in a pool of blood. At least ten rogues in various pieces were all around him. I wanted to stay and grieve, but I had no time. Valac had gotten through the portal. I leaped inside and hurried through the tunnel of fire until I reached the other side. It was hard to imagine that all of this was beneath the surface. There were hundreds of caves going in every direction.

Even this far away, I felt the eternal flame.

The muscles that had ached from the battle mended. My power grew with each step I took. The flames would have the same effect on Valac and kick-start his healing. But the injury to his arm required more than a rejuvenation of strength. He'd have to enter the external cavern to repair his broken bones. And since he'd gone hours without any tonics or herbal medicines, there was a chance the wound was already infected.

I increased my pace.

By the time I'd gotten halfway down the passageway, I was already in distress. My lungs felt as if they were collapsing, and I could only manage short breaths. Steamy air filled the tunnel, making it difficult to see. In the distance, I saw a moving shadow, and I headed for it. I couldn't run. My breathing wouldn't allow it. As I approached the hazy silhouette, I discovered it was Valac. He moved slowly, limping on one leg. The hound he'd killed at the portal must've injured him further.

I growled, and he turned around.

There was a panicked expression on his face at first. But when he noticed how I struggled for every breath, he smiled.

"You seem to be having some troubles, hound. Is the thin air down here not enough for you?"

His words enraged me, and I bared my teeth. A second later, he took off toward the end of the passageway. I sprung forward and tackled him to the ground. My paws were on his chest as he thrashed beneath me. When I bent my head toward his neck, he pulled out a small iron knife. I wasn't fast enough. He thrust the sharp edge into my ribs, and I winced from the pain. Thanks to my thicker hound skin, the blade hadn't gone deep. It was the location of the incision that caused the problem. He'd managed to cut through my ribs, and my lung fully collapsed.

I curled into a ball, and he escaped.

He glanced over his shoulder, smirking right before he entered the exterior cave that led to the eternal flame entryway. I pushed the knife out with my paw. The skin tore a little more, and I whimpered. The weapon clanged as it hit the rock flooring. I glanced down to assess the damage. The flame had already begun to heal the wound, but the lung took longer to repair. I didn't have time to wait. I managed to get on all fours and pushed myself forward. It was only a matter of time before Valac regained his power.

I had no choice.

Against my better judgment, I entered the massive external cavern. On the far end, I saw Valac crouched only a few feet away from the eternal flame's entrance. He screamed as he removed the piece of armor that had lodged into his wrist. Although I had all my strength, the limited amount of oxygen took a toll on me. As I strode toward him, I felt as if I was moving at half my normal speed. My paws were heavier, and I was dizzy. When he saw me coming for him, he stood. The shield protected his injured arm. He held an iron sword in the other. Sweat dripped down my face.

Valac swung his sword, narrowly missing my face by

inches. "You may be strong, hound. But you can't win. Not down here."

Even without Excalibur, he had some skill with the blade. We circled each other. His eyes were fixed on mine as he tried to anticipate my next move. A fire crackled all around us, while rolling balls of inferno flew out the eternal flame's entrance. I had to duck as one came right at me. Several others flew over Valac's head, briefly turning his attention away from me. It might be my only chance. Without hesitation, I pounced on him. I had him on the ground once again, but the shield protected him.

He drove his sword into my side. This time, the slice was deep. "Nice try, Marcus. But you're too late."

When he removed the blade, blood flowed out of the puncture like a river. I tried to ignore the pain as I attempted to wrestle the shield out of his hand. I was weakening rapidly, and we both knew it. I was hurt badly, and my body couldn't recover fast enough. I only had a few more seconds before he overpowered me. A shadow appeared, shimmering as the light grew. I gasped when Ariel came into view. She was barely visible, wearing a white flowing dress like some ghostly apparition. I stared at her, not believing my own eyes. She waved at me, urging me to keep fighting.

The essence she'd given me at our wedding. Had the wedding vow exchange kept her with me? It didn't matter. Knowing I still had a piece of her invigorated me. I fought back with every ounce of strength I could muster. His grip on the shield loosened, and I stripped it away from him. It scraped across the rock flooring as it slid, eventually resting against a stone pillar. He'd removed pieces of the armor while he healed. I went after the exposed skin. Blood smeared across my face as I dug my teeth into flesh and bone. I tore off the hand that wore the Ring of Dispel. His screams of agony echoed throughout the caves. The eternal flame had the power to return his hand. But the First Ones would destroy him if he tried to enter the flames. He had no other choice but to suffer the pain.

It was his turn to die.

His only defense left was the armor. As he writhed beneath me, I scratched my claws into the chest piece. It didn't even nick the metal. Last time I tried, I'd only been able to bend it. If the metal was impenetrable, I was wasting my time. There had to be a way to get it off. I had to break each section apart. Maybe if I wedged something between them, the magic protecting the armor might weaken. But I couldn't do it in my hound form. Valac was on his side, clutching his severed arm. I shifted back into my mortal form. I picked up his sword and lodged the iron between two connected parts of the breastplate. Using all my strength, I pressed the blade deeper. It wasn't working. I needed something more. We were too close to the eternal flame. Each short breath I took was harder than the last one.

I heard voices, and I swirled around. It was Selene with Ethan in his hound form. She bypassed me as she rushed to her brother's side. She went to her knees and tore off a long piece of her shirt. He moaned as she tightly tied the cloth around his wound, stopping the blood. Once she finished the tourniquet, she turned him onto his back. With his head in her lap, she said, "Take off the helmet so I can see your face."

"No." Valac reached out for her hands. "He'll kill me."

This plan was dangerous. Even in Valac's weakened state, he could hurt her. I was about to get involved when a strange feeling came over me. A wave of heat whipped through the caves. It was as if the wind were whispering in my ear, telling me not to interrupt her. The voice was calm and soothing. I hoped it was Ariel's spirit. I wanted to believe the pain from the stab wound hadn't made me hallucinate.

"You abandoned me," Valac said to Selene. "You turned against me."

"I abandoned your mission," she replied, taking his hand in hers. "I'd never abandon you."

"Did you come to rescue me?" he whimpered.

"I came to die alongside you." A tear ran down Selene's cheek. "I can feel my body aging even as we speak."

Had she heard from Rowan and Kalin? I couldn't ask Ethan because he was in his animal form. Was it all over? Guilt rushed through me. I should've stayed with them and helped in some way. But when I saw the sword hanging from the mist, I was overwhelmed with the agony of Ariel's loss. I couldn't see past my pain.

"The akasha will save us," Valac tried to assure her. "Mother told me her blood is the key."

"By the time Kalin tried, the cut was too deep," she sniffled. "The mist has fallen."

Valac lowered his hands, and she removed his helmet. "This wasn't supposed to happen. We were going to rule the courts together. It was meant to be you and me like Mother would've wanted."

"I never wanted any of this, Valac." Selene ran her hand over his cheek as blood dripped from his mouth. "I wanted to return to Avalon. I wanted to be free."

Now it all made sense. Selene and Valac were banished from Avalon when they tried to rescue Prisma from her execution. They were supposed to go to the mortal world and live out the remainder of their lives. But they were so old that they would've been dead within days. For Selene, this was all about earning her freedom. For Valac, it was something more. He pursued the fire court throne because he thought that was what Prisma had wanted. It was all about pleasing his mother.

Valac stared up at her as if he were stunned by her admission. Selene moved around his body, removing each section of the Green Armor. He didn't resist or say another word. When she finished, he wore only a pair of dark pants and a matching short-sleeved shirt. She came over to me, reaching for my hand. "He deserves to die for what he took from you, but you're right. I can't watch him suffer. I will allow you to end his life if I can ease his pain."

He ruined my life, turned elementals against their courts, caused natural disasters all over the world, and killed thousands. But for me, this was personal. I wanted him to know the unbearable ache I felt. The misery of her loss was with me in every breath I took. I deserved retribution. He owed me nothing less. "He doesn't deserve any mercy."

"If you truly feel that way, you are no better than him," Selene replied. We watched Valac curl his body into a ball, whimpering and mumbling about his discomfort. "When we forgive those who harm us, we are released from the pain. Forgiveness is the only path to peace."

The only peace I'd ever see was death. There was no going back for me. After this was over, my life no longer had a purpose. But how was I supposed to make Valac pay when he was already hurting? It would be like beating a dead horse. There was no relief if he was unable to fight back. It was obvious I'd already won. I reached down and picked up the iron knife he'd used to stab me. "I'll never forgive him for what he's done. But I won't stop you. Not for his benefit. Only for yours."

She positioned her body next to his on the rock flooring and sang a melody in his ear. Her voice was so soft I couldn't make out the song. Valac closed his eyes and smiled. He was the happiest I'd ever seen him. Ethan came to stand by my side, seemingly protecting me in case of a surprise. I went down to my knees, raising the knife high above my head. Then I plunged the iron deep in Valac's chest. His back arched, but he didn't make a sound. I pulled the blade out. The space around the incision burned and turned black, while his skin slowly turned gray. Selene moved away as his body ignited.

Within minutes, Valac was no more.

Selene's eyes welled with tears as she stared at the pile of ash. I should've walked away, given her time to grieve. But I had to know. "Everything you said back there about Kalin. Was it true?"

"No," she whimpered. "He had to believe the fight was over. Otherwise, he'd still be in that armor."

"Thank you." I wasn't sure it was appropriate, but it was all I could think of to say.

"What should we do now?" Valac's death had already taken its toll on her. The dark circles under her eyes made her look as if she'd aged ten years.

"Try to get some rest." If everything went as planned, Kalin would sacrifice herself to mend the mist. Rowan might need me during those final moments. After she was gone, I'd do everything I could to help him move forward. "I'm going to find Rowan."

CHAPTER TWENTY-TWO

KALIN

"I want to fly," I told Rowan.

His glare was curious. "You want to what?"

These last few weeks had left us very little time to ourselves. It seemed we were always needed in a council meeting or having to deal with the latest crisis within our courts. And now, we were running out of time. Soon, it would be goodbye. With that in mind, I wanted to make the most out of the time we had left together. I needed to forget about what happened for a while. "You've never taken me flying." I ran my hand over the tip of his shoulder. "I'd like to do that now."

He smirked. "Where do you want to go?"

I wanted to go everywhere. There was so much I hadn't done. So many places I wanted to visit with a certain elemental I loved, but that wasn't meant to be. "Somewhere quiet where we won't be interrupted."

Black-feathered wings shot out on either side of him. They were so large it made me wonder how he didn't fall over. He reached out for my hands, placing them around his neck. His arm went around my waist, pressing my body into his. Heat rose from the ground, collecting around my ankles. There was a tingle on the bottom of my feet. I'd read it had something to do with the magic needed to take flight. With his knees bent, he leaped up.

We were in the skies above Avalon. The wind rushed against my face and through my hair. I tightened my grip on his neck, and he chuckled. It was my first time being this high. I'd never even been on a plane. I tried not to focus on my dangling feet. Or the fact that he could drop me and I'd plunge back to the Earth like a missile. Instead, I closed my eyes and focused on the sensations all around me. It was a cloudless day. This high in the air, the temperatures were a lot cooler, almost like being in the mountains around the air court castle.

"Are you all right?" Rowan asked.

"I'm getting there." That was the most honest answer I could've given him. It was unnerving up here, but I was safe with Rowan.

I opened my eyes and took in the scenery as he flew us over the woodland territory. I was surprised to see how tall those trees were. They grew higher than the ones in the mortal world. Some of them were a dozen stories high, like mini-skyscrapers. Curious pixie faeries flew up to greet us. Their wings reminded me of butterflies as they fluttered around us. One of them tried to land on Rowan's shoulder, but he flicked him off with his finger.

"That was rude," I pointed out with a disappointed glare.

"You said you wanted privacy."

As we glided over the ocean, he dipped low enough for me to reach out and touch the cool water. It was so clear that I was able to see down into the sea. A second before he took us higher, a mermaid rose out of the water and kissed my cheek. "This is amazing," I said, resting my head against his chest.

"We're here," he replied as we landed on the white sand.

It was a small patch of beach, surrounded by forest-covered mountains. About a quarter-mile away, I saw an entrance to a cave no more than ten feet wide. "Where are we?"

"We're still in the woodland territory," he replied as he scanned the area. "Orion likes to bring Marlena here when they need some quiet time. No one will bother us, I promise."

I imagined a secluded seashore was a great getaway spot, especially if they wanted to be alone. "Have you ever been inside the cave?"

"No." He grabbed my hand, intertwining our fingers. "Do you want to check it out?"

I nodded. "Yes."

We strolled up the sand and into the shadowed entrance. Rowan ignited an orb of fire in his palm to light our way. When the cavern came into view, I gasped. Although the entryway was tiny, the rest of the space was about as large as the mountain itself. Amid the stalagmites and stalactites, crystals in a spectacular display of colors sprouted up in every direction. They ranged from miniature to the size of boulders. A transparent cave pond with constant trickling water sat in the middle of the grotto.

In my whole life, I'd never seen anything as magnificent as this place.

Rowan found a row of candles attached to the wall and lit them. "Orion was right. This place is incredible."

I ran my hand across a flat, smooth, sapphire-colored stone. "I agree."

"Let's go deeper," he suggested, with a mischievous smile.

We followed a path of flat rocks to the edge of the pond. The pink tourmaline crystals on the cave's floor gave the water a rosy glow. Across the way, I saw a large wooden chest that resembled something I'd seen in a pirate movie.

Curious, I flipped the lid open. Crocheted blankets and pillows filled the treasure box. I removed several of the largest blankets and laid them across the hard surface. Once I had sat down, I patted my hand on the space next to me, inviting him to join me.

He took off his jacket, exposing a snug-in-all-the-right-places black t-shirt. Even in the dim lighting, I saw the outline of his muscular chest and stomach. Damn, that boy wore a shirt like no other. I tried not to stare at his flexed arms while he maneuvered himself into a comfortable sitting position. As he stretched out his leather-clad legs, he leaned back onto his elbows. His ocean-blue eyes stared back at me, while his silver eyebrow piercing glinted in the light. I nearly melted into the flooring. It was no wonder he was so confident. He seemed to ooze sexiness without any effort. To him, it was as natural as breathing.

I cocked my head to the side and smiled.

"What?" he asked, with a curious brow.

Without answering, I reached for the rim of his shirt. The inquisitive expression on his face lifted as he realized what I was doing. He reached behind, yanking it over his head. My mouth was suddenly dry. The glowing light danced over his pecs, and my fingers ached to touch them. As my eyes fixated on his midsection, I noticed the beginning of the claw marks over his ribs. I ran my finger over the raised skin, and he inhaled deeply. "After you got your wings back, I figured the scars would be gone."

"I'm glad they're not." He sat up straighter, rubbing his palm over his ribcage. "They aren't my most attractive feature, but they represent everything I never want to become. Plus, it scares the shit out of anyone who sees them."

He'd gotten those scars as a punishment when he refused to kill me—my hero, in every way. "There's nothing about you that isn't beautiful," I gushed, in a dreamy tone.

"I think that's my line."

I pushed his shoulder. "I'm serious."

"I know." He tucked a loose strand of hair behind my ear. "Thank you."

Okay, this was the moment. Every nerve ending in my body sizzled, anticipating what I was about to say. I tried to settle my mind as I opened my mouth. "I know we're running out of time, and maybe it's too soon—"

"What's going on?"

The butterflies in my stomach were bouncing around like they were on a caffeine high. I leaned in, closing the distance between us. "I want you."

In an instant, his expression turned serious. "You don't have to do this. Not because of what's happening."

If the circumstances were different, maybe I would've waited. Who knows? But I didn't have that option. In a few hours, I'd be dead. But before I went, I wanted to experience this even if it was only this one time. I wanted him to know that part of me—to be part of me. "I want to do this because of you. The last gift I can give you." No chance my face wasn't beet-red. I felt the warmth in my cheeks. "I've never been with any other boy."

"I've been with other girls, but I've never been with anyone I cared about." He ran the pad of his thumb over my cheek. "This is new for me too."

I kept my eyes focused on him as I lifted my tank top over my head. I hadn't worn a bra, and I'd fought the urge to cover myself up as his eyes roamed my newly exposed skin. But I didn't. I wanted him to see me in a way no one else ever had.

"You are so gorgeous. Every inch of you is perfection." He kissed me, parting my lips with his. My heart pounded in my chest like it was trying to break through my ribs. He ran his hands through my hair, giving me goosebumps on my forearms. I lost myself in him. Breathless. He cupped his hand behind my head, lowering us both to the ground. As I relaxed beneath him, he pulled back. His eyes bore into mine. "I love you, Kalin."

"I love you too. Always." I tugged him down. He let out a low moan as he pressed his mouth against mine. At first, his kiss was so gentle that our lips barely touched. But as he unbuttoned my jeans, the kiss deepened. Things seemed to be moving in slow motion. Everything around me faded away. All I heard was our hearts beating.

And as our bodies joined, our hearts beat as one.

CHAPTER TWENTY-THREE

ROWAN

I had never known happiness like this before.

Kalin spent the last several hours wrapped in my arms. Her head buried in my chest. The strawberry scent of her hair wafted through my nose as I tried to memorize every curve of her body, every sound, and smell. I kissed the top of her head. She eventually stirred and gazed up at me with a sweet smile.

"We should probably get going," she said, arching up to kiss me. "It would be selfish to stay."

My father said his power could only hold the mist together for no more than twelve hours. If we exceeded that amount of time, the crack would grow, and the oldest elementals would start dying. At the moment, I didn't care. Kalin was about to lose her life. Sacrifice herself because I wasn't able to find another way to save her. The guilt over this had just about killed me. Once she was gone, I had no idea how I'd ever recover.

"What if you're wrong?" I questioned, praying against all the odds for the answer I wanted to hear. "The crack on the mist is small. Maybe you'll only need to use some of your blood. Maybe—"

"I'm not wrong," Kalin replied as she slipped her clothes back on. "Merlin agreed."

I rubbed the back of my neck. "How am I supposed to do this?"

She turned to face me. "Do what?"

A lump swelled in my throat. "Let you go."

"I wish it didn't have to be this way. I'd give anything to change it. But this is what I have to do." She wrapped her arms around my neck, and I tucked my head into the crook of her neck. I probably held on a little too tightly, but she didn't complain. A sharp pain grew in my chest. I was sure it was my heart breaking into a thousand pieces.

As THE SUN SET INTO THE HORIZON, WE ARRIVED AT THE SPOT OF the clash. The ground bore the scars of the battle. The pristine emerald-colored grass had been burned away in various spots, trees uprooted, and bloodstain peppered throughout the area. My stomach sank. Above our heads, we could see that the crack in the mist had grown a couple of feet. We were out of time.

Out of the corner of my eye, Britta appeared. She stepped out of the forest with her eyes fixed on the damaged mist. As she edged closer, the train of her sea-green, translucent gown dragged across the patches of dirt and burnt grass.

I reached behind, releasing Excalibur from my leather sheath. I presented the sacred artifact to her. "This belongs to you."

She twisted around, smiling when she eyed the sword. She took the weapon, and telepathically said, *"Thank you."*

I bowed my head.

A moment later, Orion and Marlena were at her side. He wore a tunic with chocolate-colored pants, while she dressed a bit more formally in an aquamarine gown drenched in gold jewelry. Since the Ring of Dispel blocked magic, they wouldn't have known about our fight with Valac. I imagined they'd had to sense the damage after he'd escaped. They both stared up at the incision. Marlena placed her fingers over her mouth as tears swam in her eyes.

Orion put his arm around her, casting a sympathetic smile. He glanced at Kalin. "I'm sorry."

"It's all right," Kalin replied, with a forced smile. "We tried our best."

There was a brief period of silence as the reality of the moment sunk in. I felt as if I were being torn apart from the inside out. There'd been moments in my life when I'd had to deal with difficult situations. Each time, I'd managed to find a reasonable solution. But not now. Not when I was the most desperate I'd ever been. I'd searched everywhere, tried everything. And nothing. As with Marcus, it made me question all I'd done. Everything we'd fought to protect and all we had lost.

Was it worth it?

Kalin had come to terms with her fate. Like she almost expected something to happen. Her selflessness was one more reason I loved her so much—one more reason I questioned my role in all of this. I was destined to end it all because I couldn't allow her to sacrifice herself. As a king of my court, I knew it was the right thing to do. It would allow us to move forward and heal what Valac had broken. But as someone who loved her, it ripped me to shreds.

"Rowan," Kalin said, breaking me from my thoughts. She pointed behind me, and I spun around.

Marcus headed toward us with a large canvas satchel over his shoulder. He made his way over to Orion, handing him the bag. He looked inside, pulling out the helmet of the Green Armor. "All of the pieces are inside, but one of the metal arms is damaged."

"How did you get it back?" Orion asked.

"Valac sustained life-threatening injuries during the final battle, and he tried to return to the eternal flame for healing. We intercepted him," Marcus said, reaching into his pocket, handing me the Ring of Dispel. "I couldn't have done it without Selene."

"Is he dead?" I asked.

"Yes," Marcus replied sternly.

We each glanced at one another with a sense of relief. The threat was over. Soon, we'd be able to balance the courts and heal the damage done in the mortal world. We'd recreate the high council, and I'd make sure the lines of communication were always open. Each of our courts had to be stronger and managed stricter. In a way, I understood my mother's firm hand in court. She'd taken things to the extreme, but her methods held our court together for centuries.

Marcus was the only one who held a blank expression on his face. He stood silent like a soldier awaiting further instruction. Taking Valac's life had given him no relief. Although he'd saved us all, he couldn't bring back the love of his life. He showed no emotion, broken after such a terrible loss. It was a feeling I would soon come to know. I glanced over at Kalin as she stared up at the mist. The moment she was gone, I'd know that emptiness he felt firsthand.

Was I strong enough to let her go?

"Kalin?" Someone shouted from a distance. I scanned the area with my hand on the grip of my sword. I'd be ready for anything. A few twigs snapped, then Kalin's mother worked her way through the thick brush. As soon as she saw her daughter, they raced toward each other until they embraced.

"What are you doing here?" Kalin asked her.

"I won't lie and say it was easy for me to accept your decision. It wasn't." Her mother wiped tears away with the back of her hand. "But I'm here now. If this is goodbye, I won't let you go through it alone."

"Thank you," Kalin replied, holding onto her tightly. "I'm glad you're here."

Once she released her mother, she made her way over to Orion and Marlene. She hugged each of them. "Thank you for being such a good friend to my father and our court."

Orion wiped a tear from his eye. "Thank you for being so brave. Your father would be proud of who you have become."

Marcus glanced away as she stood in front of him. It was as if it were painful for him to see her face. "Don't let this consume you. Ariel would've never wanted that. She'd want you to move on, no matter how difficult it may seem right now." She tilted his chin, turning his face to make eye contact with her. "I need you to promise me that you will help Rowan through this."

"I promise," he whimpered, pulling her into a hug.

The world moved in slow motion as she strode toward me. I wasn't even sure if I was still breathing. She clasped her hands on my cheeks, and I wrapped my arms around her waist. Pushing up onto her tiptoes, she kissed my lips. "I'm not sure how to say goodbye to you."

My chest ached. "I don't think I can."

Tears welled in her eyes. "No matter what happens after this, I will always be with you. Every time you feel a cool breeze against your cheek, know that it will be me."

I kissed her again, not caring that everyone watched. I needed to feel her, to take in her scent, to taste her one last time. "I love you, Kalin."

She pulled back, wiping cheeks. "I love you, too." Glancing around, she said, "I love you all."

A lump swelled in my throat as she strode toward the

mist. The crack was several yards deep now, and sparkles of magic dripped from the hole. As my father had, she stepped toward the shimmering mist. Unease crept through me. The moment I'd been dreading had come. But I wasn't ready. I couldn't, even though I knew it was right. There had to be another way. It wasn't supposed to happen. Not to Kalin. Not after everything she'd overcome, the trials, and what she'd lost. Life had never been fair, but this was torture. In an instant, I was ready to give up everything to save her. Nothing else mattered. Not even my court that I'd fought to protect. Not the lives of my friends that I knew would perish.

I sheathed my sword. "I can't do this."

"Rowan, no," Kalin replied, putting up her hand. "Please don't."

"I'm sorry, Kalin." I came to stand in between her and the mist. "I've failed my court, and even myself, but I don't care anymore. I won't let you kill yourself."

Marcus came to stand at my side. Growling, he said, "Rowan, please don't make me do this."

"There's nothing you can do to stop me." I held up my palm. Using my power, I thrust him backward. He fought for control of his body, trying to shift into his animal form. I resisted him.

A wall of water formed, separating Kalin from me. A second later, the liquid froze. I sneered at Britta. *"I won't let you kill us all, Rowan."*

Still fighting off Marcus, I placed my other hand on the wall of ice. A fire burned from my fingertips as the ice melted, more formed. Britta fought with the full strength of her power.

All of these attacks at once rapidly drained my power. I weakened by the second, but I had to hold on. I wouldn't lose Kalin. I refused to let her die.

"I'm sorry, Rowan," Orion said, spinning two large sand

tornadoes above his head. His hands thrust forward and pushed me backward.

I hit the ground with a thump, landing on my back. Pain radiated from my spine. As I got to my knees, Kalin strode into the mist. For a few seconds, I saw her shadow.

Then she was gone.

"No!" I screamed, running toward the mist.

"She's gone, Rowan. I'm sorry." Marcus said, grabbing hold of me. I squirmed in his grasp, but he wouldn't let go. "It's done."

The entire mist glowed a radiant white with a rainbow of glittering lights moving throughout. The gaping hole shimmered as it sealed back together. The incision disappeared completely, and the mist returned to its translucent tint.

Marcus released me, and I fell to my knees with my hands over my face. Soft, warm arms embraced me. It was Kalin's mother. I turned, pulling her into an embrace. Besides Marcus, she was the only other person that shared my ache. Agony rippled through me in waves. The pain was so unbearable I had to fight to take a breath. "She's gone. I can't believe it. She's gone."

"It was the only way, Rowan," Britta said, telepathically.

"Did you know this would happen?" I asked her as I tried to hold myself together.

"After Merlin was released, I received a new thread of possibility," she replied. *"I came here to see that it came to fruition."*

I looked at each person that stood around me. How did they all know exactly where we'd be and when? The woodland territory went on for miles and miles. Orion hadn't known about the fight with Valac in his territory. If he had, he would've come to our aid. But he somehow knew we'd be here now. Marcus had left hours ago without asking where we'd be. What about Kalin's mother? How had she known?

There was something they weren't telling me. "Did you summon everyone here?"

"I sent for the leaders of the other courts." She briefly glanced at Marcus. *"The hound came on his own."*

I stood, crossing my arms. "Why?"

Her pupils disappeared, and her eyes went white. She had a vision. *"There is a chance we can bring her back."*

My brief moment of happiness shifted to anger and resentment. Britta let Kalin believe there was no other alternative. She'd fought against me as I tried to keep her from entering the mist without ever revealing there was a way to save her. I scanned the faces of everyone around me. Had they all known? They each appeared as surprised as I was. I sensed she'd kept this from us all. I clenched my fists. "Why didn't you tell us?"

"I had to let the vision play out exactly as I had seen it," she replied firmly. I had no doubt she wasn't pleased by my reaction. *"If I altered even the smallest piece, I might have changed the outcome."*

Britta was right. Every choice we made could alter our future. I released the tension in my shoulders. In a calmer tone, I asked, "What did you see in your vision?"

"Kalin has made the ultimate sacrifice." Her eyes returned to their normal icy blue. *"Once the mist absorbs her power, she will be given a choice. If she returns, it will take all of us to make her whole."*

I stepped toward her. "What do we have to do?"

CHAPTER TWENTY-FOUR

KALIN

As I entered the mist, everything around me glowed white.

It felt as if I was floating on air. Something took control of my body. I tried to move, but I froze in place. My body shook like I was having a seizure. Long scratches appeared all over my arms and legs. As the wounds tore open, I screamed from the pain as blood poured out. The mist absorbed me. My vision hazed as the crimson fluid drained from my body, and I became lightheaded. My limbs sagged.

And then everything went black.

When I opened my eyes, I stood in the caverns below the air court castle. Above my head, a massive gust of wind twisted. Within the airstream, warm yellow shadows shifted around. One particular silhouette grew larger as it floated out of the wind, appearing to come toward me. The shape stood next to me and materialized into a solid form.

It was my father.

"Dad," I screamed, running toward him. He stood with his

arms opened wide. I hugged tightly around his waist. "I missed you so much."

"I'm so proud of you, Kalin." He kissed the top of my head. "You saved the world."

Gazing up at him, I asked, "Am I dead?"

"No." He pulled away, pointing into the distance. The scenery changed. We now stood on a dark flat surface surrounded by nothing but blackness. "The in-between is a reality that exists between the world of the living and the dead. Mortals refer to it as purgatory."

Had I done something wrong? I thought purgatory was a place mortals went when they wanted to go to heaven but got waitlisted instead. I reached out to touch the darkness and felt nothing. "Why am I here?"

Once again, everything around me changed. I stood in a country-style kitchen that looked similar to the one we had in my mother's house in the mortal world. A moment later, I jolted when I saw myself enter the room and sit down at a long wooden table. Several textbooks and a spiral notebook rested on the table. I appeared to be doing homework. Mom came into the room, sipping tea, and sat next to me. "What is this?"

"What you see can be your reality," he replied, with excitement in his tone.

I waved my hand in front of their faces, but neither responded. They hadn't seen me or heard us. My eyebrows furrowed as I turned to face my father. "What do you mean?"

"The mist absorbed your elemental half to heal itself, but your mortal half survived." He smiled. "Now, you must decide which future you'd like to have."

"Which *future*?" I had a hard time coming to terms with what he said. I thought I was supposed to die. There were no other options for me. How was any of this possible?

"Because of your sacrifice, you have an option to return

to the mortal world as a mortal with no memory of the elementals. Your mother will join you, and her memory of Avalon will be wiped clean."

But she'd never know the only person she ever loved. I'd never know my father. Never know my friends. Never fall in love with Rowan. "Why would I want to do that?"

"You can have the simple life you craved." He squeezed my shoulders, leveling our eyes. "You can go to college, get married, and have a child. Whatever you wish. All of the sadness and burdens you've experienced will be gone."

There were so many times I wished for that kind of life. To be able to choose my future and make my own decisions. He was offering me more than life. He was offering me a freedom I'd never known. "What's the other option?"

"You can return to Avalon as you are," he replied in a lackluster tone. It was clear which path he preferred I choose. "But, this option is much riskier."

"Why?"

"If you return, the First Wind will restore your elemental half." He rubbed the back of his neck. "In your weakened state, there is no guarantee you will survive the process."

Tension built in my shoulders. "Are you saying I could choose Avalon and still die?"

He nodded. "Yes."

This choice gave me a lot to consider, but it wasn't only about me. Many would be affected by my decision. "What will happen to my friends if I don't return? What about Rowan?"

"There will be a period of mourning," he replied, staring into the distance. "Some longer than others, but each has responsibilities within their court. They will eventually move forward with their lives."

Rowan had fought so hard for me. I thought of the last

time I saw him. The look of desperation on his face. "Will they be happy?"

"You can't make this decision based on others," he said, slightly agitated. The scenery washed away. All that surrounded us now were moving clouds. Even the surface I stood on was gone, which made me a little woozy. "This is a personal choice."

I cocked my head to the side. "It's not that simple, and you know it."

"The most important decisions are rarely simple."

I'd never been so conflicted. All of my life, I'd known where I'd be and what I was supposed to do. Now I stood at a crossroads. I could have total freedom. Live without the pain of Dad or Ariel's loss. Make my own choices. Or, I could return to Avalon. Back to the life I was destined to live. To the ones I loved. "I don't know what to do."

"We've run out of time." He took my hand in his. "What do you want to do?"

I'd given up everything to save Avalon. I'd gained and lost so much. Dad was right. For the first time, I had to think for myself. I had to decide what was best for me. The choice was clear. Now I just had to be brave enough to follow it. "I've made my decision."

CHAPTER TWENTY-FIVE

ROWAN

"*Be patient, young king,*" Britta said, telepathically.

Relief spilled over my shoulders, and I released some of the tension in my chest. Kalin was alive. That was all I needed to know. As we waited, I tried to understand what Britta had told us about her premonition. Kalin had to believe she would die. Her sacrifice had to be pure so that she would receive this gift. And now she must choose her future. But what were her choices? "You said she might come back. What was her other option?"

"*To return to the world as a mortal with no memory of the elementals,*" Britta replied, as she moved toward a small stream that ran through the area.

Without the burdens of her court, it would be a fresh start for Kalin. She'd never know the pain of Taron and Ariel's deaths. The memories of our war expunged from her memory. She'd be free.

I glanced over at Kalin's mother. "What about Tricia?"

Tricia stared at Britta. "*If Kalin chooses a mortal life, her mother will return with her.*"

"Would I have any memories of Avalon?" Tricia asked, eyes rounded.

Britta glanced at her. *"No, you would believe that Kalin's father was a soldier who died at war."*

Her eyes welled with tears. "I don't want to forget about Taron. I've spent half of my life in love with him."

Britta waved her hand. *"If you wish to return with your daughter, that is the cost."*

My heart ached for her. That was a terrible price to pay. If I had the choice, I wouldn't want to lose the memories of the one I loved. But Tricia would ultimately follow Kalin wherever she chose to go. That much I knew was true. They had been best friends since her birth. Nothing but death would keep them apart.

But what would Kalin want?

As a mortal, Kalin would design her own life. No more destiny to fulfill or life-threatening choices. Selfishly, I wanted her here. When I'd pictured eternity, I'd always hoped she'd be with me that we'd protect our courts together. But I understood if she chose to create a new future for herself. If that made her happy, I hoped she'd choose it.

Thunder filled the skies, startling us all.

I gazed up as lightning flashed. A bolt shot down, landing a few feet away from me. A thick puff of smoke covered the area. When the dust settled, I saw something lying on the ground, and I cautiously moved toward it. The closer I got, the object came into view. A lump swelled in my throat.

It was Kalin.

She'd chosen to return to Avalon. But something was wrong. Kalin wasn't moving, and her eyes remained closed. I rushed to her side with Tricia right beside me. We both fell to our knees in front of her, and I met eyes with Britta. "What's wrong with her?"

Britta pressed the palm of her hand against Kalin's chest.

"Her mortal-half survived, but she is weak. She will die if she remains in this state."

My heart was beating rapidly in my chest. "What can we do?"

"She will need a spark of power from each of the four courts." Britta glanced at each of us. *"We must give a part of our essence."*

Marlena stepped forward. A green leaf with golden trim sprouted from the middle of her chest. "This is the essence Orion gave me during our wedding ceremony. I want Kalin to have it."

"No," Orion said, stopping her hand before she could pluck the foliage from her skin. "I will give her the essence you gave me."

"You are the oldest and strongest of our kin." Marlena placed her hand over his heart. "She needs your strength more than I do."

He gently kissed her lips. "You're right, my love."

Marlena laid the leaf over Kalin's chest. A glowing light appeared all around her essence. The greenery absorbed into her chest. "Let the strength of the woodland faeries nourish you."

Britta held her hand over her chest. A tear-shaped droplet materialized in her palm. She held the water over Kalin's body. A warm light flashed as the drop landed over her heart. *"This is our gift to you, brave queen."*

With my palm over my chest, I collected my essence. It was nothing more than a single red flame. I took a deep breath and slowly blew the fire. The blaze ignited over Kalin's chest, then quickly extinguished. As she inhaled the smoke, her skin glowed. "Let this fire help you rise from the ashes."

All eyes turned to Tricia, and she put her hands over her mouth.

Panic rippled through me. Kalin had requested that her

mother reign as queen over the air court, but she was a mortal with no essence to offer. Did that mean we couldn't revive Kalin? "What are we going to do?"

The wind tickled the back of my neck, and I spun around. Marcus held out a spinning ball of air. Ariel's essence. "I can give her the essence of the air court."

A lump swelled in my throat. "Marcus, I can't take that from you. It's all you have left of her."

He shook his head as a tear ran down his cheek. "Ariel would want Kalin to have it."

I pulled Marcus into a hug. "Thank you."

I held my breath as he released the essence over her head. The wind blew through her hair, but nothing else happened. She still hadn't opened her eyes or moved even an inch. I stared at Britta. "Is there anything else?"

"We have to wait and see how her body responds," Britta replied, stepping away from us as we crowded around Kalin. *"She was frail when we began."*

Anger grew in my chest. "After everything, there is still a chance she'll die?"

A tear fell down her cheek. A rare glimpse of emotion from her normally stoic persona. *"Yes."*

My stomach churned. "Was Kalin aware that this might not work?"

"Yes." Lowering her head, she replied, *"She knowingly chose to take the risk."*

"Come on, Kalin." I took her hand in mine. An icy shiver raced down my spine. Her skin was pale and cold. "I need you to come back to me." Tricia brushed the hair away from her face with the tips of her fingers. "If you can hear me, open your eyes."

Nothing.

I laid my head on her stomach. "Please, Kalin."

Kalin's back arched, and I leaped up. Her red hair faded to

a wheat blond that matched the other air court elementals. Tricia stood and stepped backward. "What's happening?"

Wings burst out from either side of her back. Flexing wide, they were unlike any I'd ever seen. Instead of one particular kind of feather, she had a mix of all four courts. I saw scales, leaves, and even black feathers like mine.

"They're beautiful," Orion added. "Does this mean she's the akasha once more?"

As the wings relaxed at her sides, she lay flat against the grass. But she still had her eyes closed with no signs of waking up. "I have no idea," I replied. "I wasn't expecting anything like this."

"The future is always changing," Britta added. *"No matter how certain we believe it to be."*

CHAPTER TWENTY-SIX

KALIN

My eyes burst open.

The sun shone, blurring my vision. I tried to feel my way around to determine my location. There was grass in my palm, and I was lying on the ground. When my eyes came into focus, I saw my family and friends. My mother and Rowan were the closest to me. Farther away, I saw Orion, Marlena, and Marcus. I was in the woodland court, right where I'd entered the mist. When I tried to sit up, pain radiated from my back. I reached behind to touch my spine, and my fingers ran over soft feathers. I glanced over my shoulder.

Wings.

I had wings.

Was I able to move them? They flexed. Yes, I could. But they weren't like any I'd ever seen. Some of the feathers were leafy like the woodland faeries. Others scaled like the fish in the water court. As I examined them, I realized my wings represented each of the four elements. "Holy shit."

Everyone chuckled.

I stood to take a closer look, and Mom wrapped her arms

around me. "I can't believe it. I'm so happy you came back to us."

I felt the same way. When I'd stepped into the mist, I'd assumed that was the end. The premonition only said that I would die. No one mentioned I could be reborn. But what was I? "I'm as surprised as you are."

"Do you remember what happened?" Mom asked as she ran her hands over the feathers. Orion and Marlena joined her, admiring my unique wings.

I tried to piece together what had occurred after I entered the mist. All I could recall were bits of time. There was nothing that made a whole lot of sense. "I don't remember everything, but I do know Dad was there."

Mom put her hand over her chest. "What did he say?"

"I don't know." I rubbed my temple. "It's all in fragments. All I remember is that he loves us. He seemed happy wherever he was."

Mom stared into the distance as tears welled in her eyes. "Thank you for sharing that. It's a relief to know he's okay."

As she spoke, a strand of my hair fell into my face. I startled. It wasn't red. "My hair is blond? When did that happen?"

"Right before you sprouted wings," Rowan replied, as he fiddled with one of my curls. "I think it's hot."

"Does that mean I'm an air elemental?" I asked.

I glanced at Britta. *We revived you using a piece of each of our essences, and now you are pure elemental.*

"Is that any different than what I was before?" I questioned.

You were half-mortal then. I suspect you are stronger now.

I saw a flash of light. Images I recognized came into view. Islands were being torn apart by massive winds, hurricanes swirled in the water, and tornados whipped across farmland.

There was devastation all over the mortal world. In an instant, I knew what I must do. I spread my wings and burst into the air, passing through Avalon's mist. I flew hundreds of miles in the air, then stopped. My wings flapped, holding me in place.

I called to the elements.

Rowan flew next to me with his black wings flapping heavily. "What the hell are you doing?"

I had the answer. My purpose was clear, like never before. "I have the power to stop the devastation." I put my hand over my heart. "I feel it growing inside of me. I have to help the mortals. I must protect them."

"I want to help you."

"You can't," I replied, shaking my head. He didn't look convinced. "Trust me, okay?"

He stared at me as if he was preparing to put up a fight, then he sighed and glided back down to the ground.

The elements tugged at me, sensing my power. I tried to steady the unrest. I was stronger in my pure form. Energy flowed in and out of me with ease as I slowly calmed the natural disasters plaguing the mortal world. One by one, they subsided. But I knew I could do more. I focused on all of the destruction. Trees sprouted out of the burned ruins. Crops of fresh fruits and vegetables regrew in the flooded plains. Glaciers returned to their icy lands. Without any drain of power, I renewed the world.

When I sensed the balance had returned, I returned to Avalon. Rowan was the only one that remained. "Where did everyone go?"

"They went back to their courts when Britta told us you had restored the balance. Tricia asked that you return to the air court when you can."

"We did it, Rowan." I wrapped my arms around his neck. "It's finally over."

"No, Kalin." He pressed our bodies together until there was no space left between us. "You did it. You saved us all."

I thought of Ariel and Dad. "Not everyone."

"That's true." He tucked a loose strand of hair behind my ear. "But you saved more than you lost. That has to count for something."

In the scheme of things, it did. We'd loved and lost, rejoiced and cried. That was all part of life. I had no idea what the future held for me, but I'd discovered a few things along the way. Avalon was where I belonged. I was destined to live this life. I was who I was supposed to be. I'd spend the rest of eternity keeping the balance, and I was proud to be its chosen protector.

I leaned in and kissed Rowan.

"What was that for?" he asked, smirking curiously.

"I'm happy," I replied, sensing all the peace around me. "I'm finally free."

ACKNOWLEDGMENTS

There have been so many people who have helped me throughout my journey. The first in a long line is my parents, Russell and Brenda Howell. I really cannot say enough about them. They've always supported and encouraged me to follow my dreams. None of this is possible without them. I want to send out a special thank you to my husband, Christopher. Every book I've written has come with some drama. You have kept my life going during the process. Thank you for dealing with me and all my crazy. You're full of awesome! Big hugs and kisses to my daughter, Madison. You'll never know how much I love you. Having you has been the greatest joy of my life. Najla Qamber certainly deserves a big hug for the beautiful book covers. You blow my mind every time. I can't go without mentioning my family and friends who have been pimping this series. You know who you are. I want you to know I appreciate your support. Thank you to all the bloggers who have read and reviewed my books. Whether you liked them or not, you picked my books out of thousands, and I thank you! You've been a huge part of my success, and I cannot tell you how much that means to me. I heart you so much! Last, but not least, I want to thank you—the reader. Your reviews, tweets, and emails continue to touch my heart and sometimes even bring me to tears. Thank you for choosing my series. These books have been a labor of love, and I truly appreciate your support. Big, awkward virtual hug coming your way. ;-)

ABOUT STACEY

Stacey O'Neale lives in Annapolis, Maryland. When she's not writing, she spends her time fangirling over books, blogging, watching fantasy television shows, cheering for the Baltimore Ravens, and hanging out with her husband and daughter.

Her career in publishing started as a blogger-turned-publicist for two successful small publishers. Stacey writes young adult paranormal romance and adult science fiction romance. Her books always include swoon-worthy heroes, snarky heroines, and lots of kissing.

Stacey loves hearing from readers. Follow her on Twitter, Facebook, Instagram, Bookbub, and Amazon. You can also join her Goodreads group, Stacey's Squad. Visit her blog at http://staceyoneale.com/.

facebook.com/AuthorStaceyONeale

twitter.com/StaceyONeale

instagram.com/staceyoneale

bookbub.com/profile/stacey-o-neale

SUMMARY

The explosive conclusion to Stacey O'Neale's award-winning Mortal Enchantment series reveals the secrets of the fantasy world!

Valac has stolen two of the sacred objects. In a bid to rule all four courts, he has threatened to use Excalibur to cut the mist that protects Avalon--ultimately ending the lives of thousands of elementals. As the Akasha, Kalin has the power to stop him. And she refuses to lose anyone else she loves.

Will she have to sacrifice herself to save them?

Desperate to save Kalin's life, Rowan searches for the long-lost creator of the mist. But what he finds is the very last thing he expected. Everything he thought he knew about his past is turned upside down, and he questions whether he's meant to be the savior or the elemental that destroys them all.

Told from Kalin, Rowan, and Marcus's perspective, the final installment to the series follows their journey of courage, duty, sacrifice, and love.

22002112R00136